# Confessions of a Cyber Girl

## BRISTOL WEDGEWOOD

Archway Publishing books may be ordered through booksellers or by contacting:

Archway Publishing
1663 Liberty Drive
Bloomington, IN 47403
www.archwaypublishing.com
1 (888) 242-5904

ISBN: 978-1-4808-3989-2 (sc)
ISBN: 978-1-4808-3990-8 (e)

Library of Congress Control Number: 2016918879

Print information available on the last page.

Archway Publishing rev. date: 11/11/2016

# *Acknowledgments*

I wish to thank all who encouraged me and supported my decision to create a compilation of my art and stories for publication—specifically, Lionel, Gerald, Snosken, Alexa, Javier, Junea, Will, Muroi, Figaro, Nelson, Vanessa, Donna, Richard, Samodiro, Robert, Matt, Dienara, David, Andy, Judy, Wooly, Mikey, Brett, Kita Dove, Nathan, Keisha, Kurt, and Tim.

# *Introduction*

My name is Vantessa. I claimed that name as my unique fantasy character years ago, and I never outgrew it. Often, I have walked a thin line between my normal (vanilla) lifestyle and my fantasy life. Where the two meet is the challenge. On occasion, I have crossed the line. This is my story, and it is accompanied by my original artwork.

A series of significant emotional events shaped me. This book reveals my humble beginnings as a young person and progresses to my twenties. It doesn't end there. In many ways, my journey to becoming a cyber girl was only just beginning.

We begin in my hometown of Bronx, New York, and travel to the foggy California coast. From there, we shall venture to Florida and then to other places far out of this world! The beautiful thing about the future is that it has so many possibilities. As the title of this book suggests, I became a cyber girl.

I became fascinated with certain behaviors regarding adult situations at an early age. The pieces of the puzzle are many and varied. I guess I just discovered something that I didn't really understand. It was an awakening. Quite simply, I experienced a sexual "thou shalt not do," and I enjoyed it too much to stop. It pulled me like a magnet. In the strangest of circumstances, I felt the pure delight of submissive obedience and surrender. It turned out to be more than just a pleasurable tendency. The nature and result of my sexual cravings have continued to influence me throughout adulthood. Once again, I reflect on the purely coincidental, insignificant events in my life that have rocked my world. The beginnings of my journey are hereby laid bare. Please enjoy!

Yes! It is me, Vantessa!

# Table of Confessions

# *Early Beginnings of a Cyber Girl*

I was born on September 25, 1975 and grew up in a government-subsidized modular apartment near Castle Hill Avenue in South Bronx, New York.

I was a fairly normal kid growing up in an emerging yet rundown borough outside the Big Apple. I grew up naturally inquisitive. An average student, I stayed away from drugs and fights, resisted the urge to shoplift, and learned how to run, climb fences, and shoot hoops. I prided myself on being willing to try new things but also avoid trouble on the volatile streets of Fort Apache. I wasn't a tomboy, but I was athletic. On my own, I grew up with a deep appreciation of art and music. I was also a late bloomer. At age fifteen, I finally began to look less girlish and more like a young woman. By the time I reached sixteen, I had a slender figure and ample breasts. Many of the boys teased me or did things like punch me in the arm to try to get me to notice them.

As an average student, school was more of a prison to me than a place to develop my mind. In class, most kids constantly goofed off or played with their personal electronic devices. The Internet was in its infancy. My teachers were pretty much hamstrung by the system, as they were unable to compete with the constant barrage of increasing disruption and electronic input. I was bored. I preferred to go to the library and read up on interesting subjects. Mythology, science fiction, and suspense thrillers were my drugs.

I liked to draw pictures and create my own stories and fantasies to escape the mundane reality of a standard public education. My favorite subjects to draw were superheroes, caricatures of my teachers, and even nudes. I once made the mistake of showing some friends my etchings. They elicited quite a few giggles and negative comments. After seeing my drawings, some of my friends commented that I might someday be a famous artist. I hoped so and thought, *Well, maybe someday.*

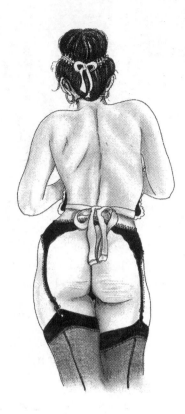

Mom had earned her stripes that day.

I wasn't a loner but kept mostly to myself and a few close friends. I created and interacted with an imaginary cast of detectives, secret agents, warriors, superheroes, and villains in my own worlds—my escape clause, if you will.

I was raised in a single-parent household for the most part. Even though we lived hand-to-mouth, we got by, and my mother, Alexa, tried her best to make ends meet. I have to give her credit. She was a soulful provider and my dearest friend and adviser. She always had the words I needed to hear. We were a team.

Growing up in America's largest city can get hectic. Whenever I became depressed or bored, I would just take a small vacation into one of my fantasy worlds. I was lucky because I was able to instantly retreat into imaginary scenes. There I could control events, be anyone, and do almost anything. I used to make up mini-adventures while riding on the L and revisited the steamier sequences in my mind frequently. It was my way of coping with a restless imagination and the mundane insanity of daily living. Best of all, no one knew of the adventures I had secretly conjured up. Always the damsel, I was captured, lured, or entrapped by evil-minded villains.

My mother was born and raised in the slums of Puerto Rico. Being a pretty girl, she found work as a hostess at a local beach bar and grill. She was only sixteen at the time. That is where my father, a Navy man of Korean dissent, discovered her. They were both swept off their feet. The whirlwind romance was right out of a movie and led her to citizenship and a life in New York. Mom was eighteen when I was born. She is still a nicely-shaped woman. Barring the effects of gravity, she is very attractive, and I am fortunate to have her genes. Two years after my birth, my father passed on from an undiagnosed medical condition.

Mom and Uncle Johnny

# The Incident: First Confession

One Sunday morning, I was in my room, finishing my homework, when my mom walked out to the kitchen to make pancakes. The man staying over came out a few moments later. I watched through my partly opened door as a verbal exchange quickly turned into an altercation. She was angry with her boyfriend, John. (She called him my uncle Johnny.) I was introduced to him, but I really didn't interact with any of mom's boyfriends.

Uncle Johnny worked at an auto body shop a few blocks away. I accepted the fact that my mother had boyfriends. It was only natural. Johnny was, for lack of a better description, the flavor of the month. Adults interacted differently, and they knew what they were doing, right? I was only eight years old at the time.

On this particular Sunday, the argument quickly became heated. I was watching their body language through the small opening of my bedroom door. I could not quite understand what they were saying but watched the scene unfold from my bedroom. Mom was wearing her three-quarter-length house robe, like she did most mornings. She had just prepared the pancake batter and was about to begin pouring it into the pan.

During the yelling match that ensued, Mom made a gesture and threatened to hit him with the pancake flipper. She was definitely angry about something. The man was equally angry and physically stronger. His body language looked menacing. I watched the scene in slow motion, a helpless bystander. Mind you, this was all happening during what should have been a quiet weekend breakfast. They both ignored the fact I was home and most likely listening to their altercation. I was genuinely afraid for my mom and thought about calling the police. She didn't back down and took a few swats at him.

Vantessa learned the hard way.

I was very young and totally freaked out as I watched Mom's beautiful red terrycloth robe pulled open by the furious man. Her chest was exposed, and I could see she was nude underneath. Mom's breasts are like firm peaches, and they swayed wildly like water balloons. My world changed. I couldn't stop watching the developing spectacle and stayed in my room.

I didn't really know what he was capable of. With all the finesse of a professional wrestler, he spun her around, removed the robe, and flipped her face-down onto the sofa over his lap. He easily pinned one arm behind her back to get her under control. She bounced like a rag doll as I watched the scene unfolding before me.

After a brief moment, she used one arm to support herself on the sofa as he began to slap her naked bottom with the very same pancake flipper she had struck him with. He kept her writhing form under control and began to vigorously spank her like a naughty child. I had a feeling that my life was never going to be the same. My hand was on the telephone, but I just froze with fascination.

I watched in shocked disbelief as this strange man, in ritualistic fashion, spanked my naked mom's butt with her own pancake flipper. She flailed, squirmed, shrieked, and cried out every time the pancake flipper stung her butt. He stopped and whispered something in her ear. I couldn't hear what Johnny was saying, but my mother kept saying, "Yes, *papi!* Yes, *papi!*" Then she began counting each stroke aloud. Holding her right wrist to her back, he continued to methodically spank her. I silently counted each stroke of that spatula in unison with her. My eyes were glued to the exhibition in the next room.

Thank you, *papi!*

Mom gasped and cried out the number of strokes as if this were some ritualistic event between them. I wondered if she had done this before. He then set to work with that pancake flipper. *Smap! Slap! Whap!* She took a vigorous whipping on her naked butt. Her shapely bottom turned bright pink and then angry red.

I watched as my mom wiggled like a worm on a hook, now gasping with the impact and moaning out the number of strokes: "Twenty-one, twenty-two, twenty-three ..."

I was devastated by what my eyes saw, but what happened next affected me more than the corrective spanking itself.

While smacking her bottom, Johnny kept asking her questions to the effect of, "Are you going to be a good girl from now on? Alexa, are you going to be a good girl?" *Smack! Smack! Smack!*

She cried out, "Twenty-four, twenty-five, twenty-six … yes, *papi*." I was distressed to witness my mother taking punishment like a naughty child. I had never seen her act like this. This was a side of my mother that I had never known. I began to question everything I thought I knew.

I don't remember if I was crying, screaming, or silently holding my breath. I was glad I was not involved in the fracas. After the spanking session, he nonchalantly shoved her forward, rolling her down his legs onto the floor. Mom plopped onto the floor like a bag of trash. *Wump!* Vigorously rubbing her red-striped bottom, mom looked up. Eyes brimming, she cried out, "Yes, *papi!*"

He loved me and spanked me.

Next, he barked at her to stop rubbing her sore butt and stand up. Like an obedient pet, mom halted instantly on command. Her naked bottom looked like it had been perched on a hot barbeque grill. She awkwardly steadied herself, and then they embraced like lovers once again. I was relieved the punishment had stopped. I saw her freshly spanked bottom glowing from the mistreatment.

Trying not to rub her burning bottom, she forlornly embraced him. He whispered something to her, and they French kissed each other long and passionately.

I could see remnants of her eye makeup streaking down her face. She was quietly resigned, looking downward as he held her for several seconds. He then used a soothing tone of voice. "There now, just be a good girl, Alexa." They held each other some more as he ran his hands all over her now glowing, naked booty. He wasn't rubbing the fire out so much as enjoying mom's hot, shapely rump.

He then raised his hand up in front of her face, offering it to her, and she obediently leaned in. I will never forget what happened next. She reached up with both hands, holding it, and placed her lips on it lovingly. She ardently licked and kissed the very hand that had just welted her bottom side.

To my total disbelief, she then apologized and thanked him for the corrective therapy. "Sorry, *papi.*" They embraced once again, holding each other, whispering like lovers.

"Good girl, Lexa! Now go and cook breakfast for me! Go." She turned and received one more playful swat on her backside, trotting off smartly as he dismissed her. The argument was over.

I was crestfallen. Watching my mother take a licking like a trained poodle and then kiss and lick the hand that had whipped her bottom was too much! Perhaps, when all was quiet, I would quickly sneak outside for a while. My world had been turned on its head. Everything I thought I knew had been swept away.

I came out of my room a few moments later, and everyone acted like nothing had happened. As I sat down to eat my hotcakes, Mom and Uncle Johnny retreated to the bedroom once again for what seemed like a really long time (though it may have only been fifteen minutes or so).

Mom emerged from the bedroom cleaned up, but I knew she was still wearing the red marks on her backside. She wore her robe and served me two more fresh, golden-brown pancakes with butter and syrup.

Attitude improvement

I sat quietly, eating and watching cartoons. She quietly told me to eat my breakfast and then go outside. She gave me explicit instructions to walk around the entire complex at least three times before coming back home. It was an unusual request, but I didn't question my mom—not after witnessing her sordid chastisement.

As I silently ate my pancakes, I didn't know what to think about what I had just observed. Was she aware that I saw everything? Did it matter? Was this what I had to look forward to as an adult female in the world?

My mom was my best friend, my security; she was everything safe, protective, and good in my life at the time. I silently reviewed the scene again and again as I strolled around the block. The images of her arms pinned behind her as she was given an old-fashioned, over-the-knee spanking replayed like a looping nightmare. It was surreal. After her chastisement, she worshipped her master's hand. Was this the way of things? Or was it something worse? Did she enjoy it? Did she actively seek out this kind of treatment?

While I ate my breakfast, she once again disappeared into her bedroom. I reflectively wondered how mother had become like a broken record. It was as if I had learned a dark and secret lesson of life. Life abruptly became more complicated as I began to question what relationships with members of the opposite camp were all about. I felt less secure.

I contemplated the scene in my mind as I strolled. I could not stop thinking about what I had just witnessed as I walked around the projects only twice (not three times). It was a cold, drizzly autumn day. None of my friends were around. I wanted to talk to someone but wasn't sure if I should. When I went back inside, it was quiet, and the bedroom door was again shut. It was a weekend, and Mom liked to sleep late on weekends. I was pretty young at the time, and I didn't fully understand what I had just witnessed. At the conclusion of my abbreviated walk around the complex, I reasoned that this was merely mom's way of engaging in love. Mom's passion increased after taking her punishment.

Warm afterglow

It never occurred to me that she was having a special sexual relationship with this man. I had heard about kids seeing porn on the monitor and how "white stuff" comes out of a man's penis. I knew that some people used whips and chains for their sexual exploits, but I didn't think too much about such things.

After my walk, I went back to my room and listened to some music for a moment. All was quiet. Then I turned on a movie and tried to not think about what I had witnessed.

Since that event, I learned that men have the power to get what they want. They are physically stronger. They sometimes help pay the bills. These were the facts of life that I felt in total agreement with. My mother and this man had something between them—a mutual understanding.

My mother worked by day at a nearby restaurant but was also quietly making money on the side. Living in New York City is an expensive proposition. The promises from elected government officials rendered a meager 21 percent of our basic living expenses. A single-parent household in most places is challenging enough, but in the Big Apple, it can be a struggle for survival. My mother had a real challenge making our household money last before the month ran out.

I later discovered how mom truly made her extra money. I came home early one day (after a half day of school), peeped into mom's bedroom, and saw her naked on her knees, performing fellatio on a neighbor man. I immediately ducked away, ran to my room, and quietly closed the door. They were not aware of my presence. I heard mom name the price, accept payment, and confirm an appointment for next week. It was then I understood that she did sexual favors for money to help make ends meet. It helped put food on the table. I still do not fault her for that.

# Villain's Convention: Confession #2

My first experience with a tingling in the pit of my belly hit me with an unexpected impact. I was nine years old. My latent submissive nature emerged as a result of finding an old, worn-out, classic comic book at the local laundromat. It was beat-up and had no cover. I was just about to toss it into the severely corroded trash when I realized I had time to kill. I had to wait for the laundry to complete its cycle in the dryer, so I picked it up and began flipping through the discarded rag.

In this particular classic issue, the famously featured Amazon superheroine was collectively weakened by three supervillains as they worked their treachery on her. They used deception to weaken and defeat her. Each of the vile men was hell-bent on winning a coveted Golden Award, similar to an Oscar. All they had to do was capture her, render her helpless, and bring her to the grand theater at the secret International Villains Convention. Once paraded onstage, she would be displayed like a trophy. The award and all of its accolades would be the mantelpiece for the mastermind who had reduced her to a captive exhibit.

This was very exciting stuff! I read the comic a few more times. I pocketed the riveting book and took it home with the basket of clothes. I didn't realize it then, but it stimulated me in a sexual way. There was something about seeing the great Amazon herself—so majestic and beautiful—degraded and ultimately taken down by a six-inch-tall supervillain. She was helpless and then paraded on stage like a pet on a leash. I got quite an electric buzz from the pit of my belly to the place between my legs when I read how the criminal audience exulted while the statuesque superheroine was placed on display—and by a six-inch man! I now find the symbolism to be quite amusing.

By age twelve, I knew what sex was all about. I sometimes heard Mom getting down with her boyfriends. Mom's passionate lovemaking was no secret when she moaned aloud with intermittent slapping sounds emanating through the closed door. I surmised that she was spanked regularly before or during sex. I understood now. I felt desire, too.

At night, I used to fantasize and imagine all kinds of traps a captured superheroine or princess could get herself into. I used to pretend I too was a superheroine and many times felt a tingle in the pit of my belly. One night, that feeling suddenly shot electric bolts between my legs as the plot thickened.

He was fascinated by my boobs.

Corrected

Was I reliving an experience similar to my mom receiving corporal punishment? Being dominated was a high. My mother certainly seemed to accept that she deserved correction. I recently found out that mom still regularly seeks out this kind of treatment. She took her medicine stroke by stroke, carefully keeping count. Then she kissed the hand that had disciplined her. It was a form of foreplay. I started to see a pattern developing.

When playing with my friends and kids in the neighborhood, I was the girl who played the role of kidnapping victim, helpless cowgirl, or captive princess tied to the chair. My friends, after a time, noted this tendency while we were at play and ridiculed me for it. It was not acceptable behavior in the neighborhood. They shrugged it off as if I were some kind of freak. Therefore, I had to keep my cravings to myself. I did keep my desires bottled up for a long time after that. It was my secret place. I no longer cared if it was unnatural or not. It was delicious, and I could not deny it.

One such night, I was fantasizing that I was abducted by a group of evil warriors on a lost exotic tropical island. I was paraded and humiliated by a clan of primitive men. As I was held prisoner, I looked down out of a hanging cage in the great hall of their mountain cave hideout. I fantasized that I was made to wear a sexy leopard skin loincloth. I was ordered to do simple humiliating tasks for the amusement of my captors. It turned me on. Being humiliated and degraded by a group of short, primitive subjugators was only the beginning.

I visualized being kept a slave girl by this band of faceless native males. I was stripped and examined up close. It made me tingle. I developed this heavy Freudian freeform story lying awake at night while instinctively rubbing myself—and then "it" happened.

When I rubbed my thighs together and used my fingers just below my pubic mound, something happened. Something was etched in my brain that made my fantasy scenario even more pleasurable and intense. I started to experience what I would later find out was my first orgasm. It was a blood-pounding, pulsing hunger emanating from the core of my pelvic region. It built up until it burst into a shower of sparks and a floating sensation after the fireworks faded. I wanted to repeat it again and again—and I did. After that first time, there was no stopping me. My imagination knew no bounds, and I found I could slip into my fantasy world, relive an experience, or pick up the storyline where I had left off. I invented many different stories all ending in unique but similar results.

Until then, I didn't know what an orgasm was, but this experience was a good, warm feeling. It relaxed me. I felt peaceful and ready to achieve this new climax again. I could do it anytime, anywhere I liked, undetected. I spoke to no one of this new discovery, thinking it was probably evil or deviant in some way. It also got me into hunting for and purchasing many more classic comic books and erotic literature. It never occurred to me how I might react to male domination in real life. Enter Morris Beckley.

Stimulating proposition

Alexa wants to be a good girl.

Stress testing

# Beckley: Confession #3

There were not many white students in our neighborhood or at school, but there was one such boy. His name was Beckley. Rough around the edges, Beckley was a pale-skinned hood rat with strawberry blonde hair, sporadic facial hair, and blue, golf-ball-size eyes. It was just an oddity, really. When I saw him at school, he was usually in trouble and being escorted by the dean. I intuitively knew that he practiced negative behaviors in order to gain acceptance by his peers. He wanted to be a gangster. I believe it is a malady now commonly known as adaptive inferiority. He wanted approval and to fit in. It was all about validation.

He was a poor white kid and used to get picked on and beaten up by other boys at school. One day, he decided he had had enough. It was a Friday near the end of the school year. He put several metal rings on his fingers, took position near a carefully selected stairway, and waited for his latest tormentor to walk down.

When his target bully descended the stairs, Beckley ran at full force and monkey-punched the bully in the back of the head, knocking the unsuspecting target down. Beckley was rumored to have done this particular maneuver at least four times, and word got around, "Don't mess with the white kid, or he will do the *swoop* on you." The swoop? Someone even gave his vengeful maneuver a moniker.

He was not very tall; he was unkempt and not athletic or charismatic at all. I met him on the street once while skipping class. We walked the snowy streets to Park Chester and went into a corner grocery store. I bought a comic book, and Beckley stole a package of gum. We then got a slice of pizza and soda before returning to a late afternoon class period. I learned that we were both only fourteen. I played stickball with him on the opposing team. His athletic performance was not very impressive.

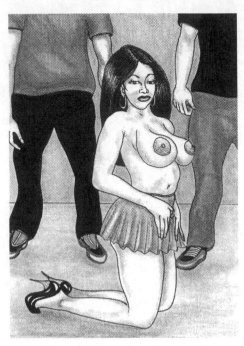

Learning to play the game

Two and a half years later, as I was walking home on Zerega Avenue, Beckley walked across the street to talk to me. "Hey, Beckley," I greeted him. He smiled, reached out, and abruptly just grabbed me by my nipples. His pinch went right through my sweater, blouse, and bra. His thumb and index finger homed in on them like heat-seeking missiles, and he held me like that. It didn't hurt.

It happened so fast, I just stood there. I still remember the feel of that grip. I was immobilized and let him hold onto my nipples. It was an exceedingly pleasurable experience—and it was risky. I didn't even think about the public spectacle we surely made out in the open. I did nothing to stop him. He really didn't know me that well. Yet here he was, touching me intimately—and on the street, no less.

He certainly had nerve! It wasn't painful, but it did stir a feeling deep inside me. It felt good to be manhandled like this. I didn't move to stop him. It was electric. I surrendered.

He just held me like that for what seemed like forever. The longer I stood there, the more energized I felt. I stared into his robin's egg blue eyes as he squinted. The look on his face was that of curiosity, as if he were trying to find out what was going through my mind at the time. He expertly used just enough force on my nipples to pull me into a deep, soulful kiss. It is strange what one remembers about such events in their lives. I remember that moment like it was five minutes ago. He pulled me by my tits just like that so he could kiss me. He gently twisted and tugged on my nubile buds while inserting his forceful, wagging tongue inside my mouth.

Secret laboratory of an evil genius

Feeling free and easy

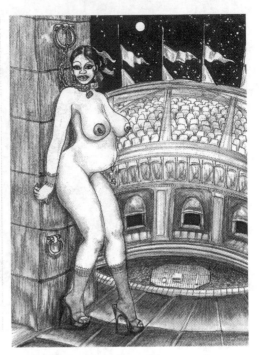

Superheroine Vantessa about to get
corrective therapy

Captured and awaiting auction

It was rapture. Beckley kneaded my breasts like dough while our tongues playfully intertwined and slid around one another. It was a tremendous rush to be kissed like that, in broad daylight, regardless of the consequences. At that moment, I was falling for him. The sensation was new and exhilarating, and it stirred me.

We were the same age, but he was more knowledgeable and experienced than I was. Mom had once explained the birds and the bees, and it all seemed rather silly and mildly disgusting to me. When Beckley latched on, I just opened my mouth, closed my eyes, and let him kiss me. Time stood still.

This encounter was the first time I had passionately French-kissed a boy. It was a delightful new experience, and I tried to keep up. Our eyes were closed. All the while, his hands expertly tweaked and gently kneaded my nipples. It felt delicious. If it is indeed possible, then a most amazing thing happened—my tongue orgasmed. Yes! It really happened! It felt buzzed with energy. I discovered later on that nearly every part of the human body is a potential erogenous zone. In other words, every part of the human body is indeed capable of orgasmic sensations.

I melted under his touch as we continued our osculation. I tried to wag my tongue as quickly and forcefully to keep up. I didn't want to let on that I was a novice kisser. I wanted to wrap myself around him. Where was this tingling feeling all of my life? Holy cow! Whatever this was about was better than reading erotic literature. I felt the blood rushing and my heart pound in my chest, all the way to my core.

The kissing was so stimulating, I almost gushed. He was wearing cologne, and I smelled it on my pillow later that night. It stimulated my senses, and I wanted even more of this treatment. To this day, I still get a flash of that moment when I get a whiff of that cologne. It's amazing that a simple presence of a fragrance or scent can trigger a response like that.

Breaking off the kiss yielded a collective sigh between us.

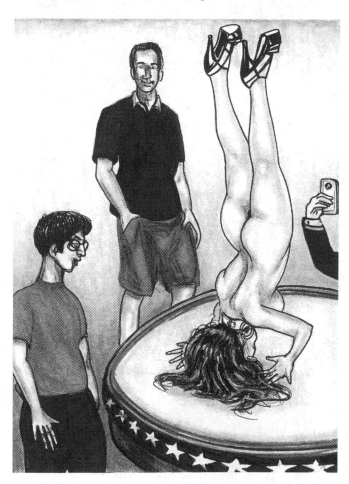

Standing on her head for their amusement

In the crawlspace

My first reaction to Beckley's indecent advances should have been to slap him and run away, but instead, I let it happen. What did that say about me?

I suddenly believed that I had been challenged. It was obvious Beckley was an experienced lover. He was brazen and wanted me to respond. In a split second, I let myself slip into a submissive role, which is what he was hoping for. He later told me in another intimate moment how he just knew "I would make a great submissive slut." Beckley was going to show me.

Most girls I knew boasted of how they could perform fellatio like it was some rite of passage. I didn't understand the attraction, but I began to get an inkling of this new domination and submission game. Beckley was about to explain the rules. It felt so good to be controlled and handled. I practically gushed when he put his hands on me. I was just beginning to learn what my dear mother already knew and practiced. She relished chastisement prior to making love.

Beckley and I looked into each other's eyes as he released my tits. He looked concerned and loving. I felt like he could have ripped my blouse open, right then and there, and I wouldn't have cared. We were past the point of no return now.

With a wink of his eye, he handed over his key and whispered to me, "Go up into my flat. Go in the bathroom, take off your clothes, and prepare a bath for us." I nodded, still dazed and buzzed from the passionate, extended kiss. I was captivated by this new feeling. I wanted to please him and for him to touch me some more. Eye contact signaled nonverbal cues. My stomach was filled with butterflies knowing he was going to touch me again.

As I turned to carry out his request, I felt a sharp smack on my bottom, goading me to trot ahead and to hurry up and carry out my orders—exactly the way I remember my mother doing years earlier. I took it affectionately.

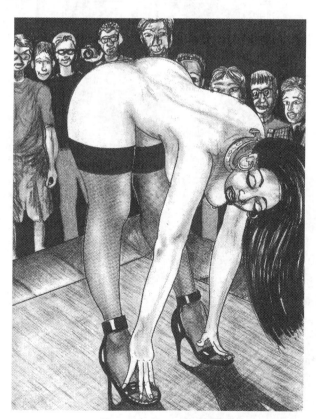

Showing her goodies

Hanging out

I had made out twice before with guys, but this was my first true sexual encounter. I should have been frightened out of my wits by this sudden behavior, especially because of the way it was initiated. So many things could have gone wrong. But I was not afraid. And the swat on my behind reminded me of Mom. I was now being a good girl and wanted to see what was next!

The pattern was set. This was a whole new playground. I began to feel much more grown up. I felt fresh, naughty, and alive! This wasn't just playing doctor; this was something grander and more thrilling.

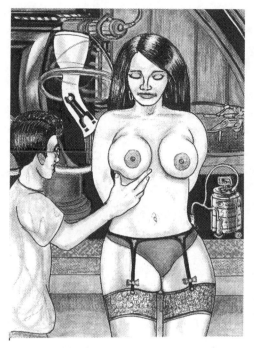

Breast examination

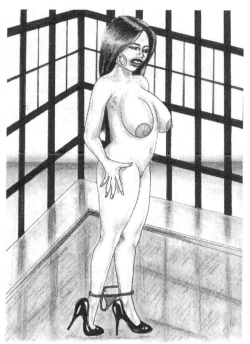

Caged and exposed

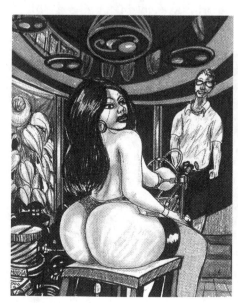

Testing her elasticity

I poured way too much bath oil, and the tub overflowed with suds. After stripping down, I climbed into the tub and waited for him. I was so excited by the prospect of being naked in the tub with him. Even stranger, it was with Beckley, of all people. What were the odds?

Some would argue that I should have just run out of there and told my mother everything. To this day, I do not know why I didn't. I took a huge gamble by going further with Beckley. The promise of further sex play with Beckley was too irresistible to me to stop. I wanted it immediately!

The water was just the right temperature, or so I guesstimated. It felt natural. I stole glances in the mirror as I inspected myself. I tied my hair back and refreshed my lip gloss once more. I heard footsteps coming to the bathroom door. My heartbeat picked up. My nipples became erect, like they were being pulled by some kind of magnetic field. Could they sense his presence? It felt like it.

Would he like me? Did I look too plain? Was my pubic hair too thick? All kinds of crazy thoughts flashed through my head. I had butterflies in the pit of my belly, and I was on the edge. I wanted him to touch me in my intimate places. I still felt the afterglow of the curbside kissing event. I felt punch-drunk and couldn't wait for him to kiss me and maybe cup and squeeze my bare breasts again. I was not only going to let him, but also rub my bare skin against him until he took charge of me. Maybe he would like to taste them. I wanted him to be my primitive caveman and to be his girl. I was acting like a hussy! What on earth was wrong with me?

In the backyard with the guys

I couldn't wait for him to cup and squeeze my breasts again.

The door opened, and Beckley walked in wearing only a blue and white beach towel. Beckley was gentle and kissed me passionately on the lips again. I felt a surge of energy in my stomach as together we sank into the bubbles and kissed. A few moments later, in slow motion, I saw it! I noticed that his pubes were also a dishwater blonde color. He was indeed a natural blonde. It was fascinating. He asked me to wash him, and I took the soapy sponge and started at his neck, watching the bubbles slide down his chest. With bath bubbles clinging to my bosom, I gently washed his arms and shoulders. I started softly kissing him as I worked my way down until he asked me if I wanted to play "submarine pens." I just smiled, not really knowing what he meant. We kissed for a long time once again, and I suddenly felt more than ready to play submarine pens with him.

Beckley had me straddle him in the plethora of bubbles. I felt his excitement as his turgid member poked me while he fondled my breasts. He used his left hand to position himself at the entrance of my grotto. We were about to play submarine pen.

My first wet sexual experience was in that tub. The first time he tried to penetrate me, he awkwardly poked the wrong orifice, and we both had a good laugh about that. We covered each other with bubbles, kissed passionately, and then came the supreme moment when he entered me. Ahhhhh! Oh! It was better than I ever imagined. We were connected where boy truly meets girl. In the privacy of my bedroom, I had masturbated using a few various objects, but this was so much better. It was a divine feeling, and I fit him like a glove.

With him inside me, we continued to kiss passionately. Soapy bubbles ran down our bodies, and he kissed and suckled on my blossoming tits. I instinctively began to hump his male appendage, engulfing as much as I could until my vagina adjusted to his length and girth. It didn't hurt, but it did take several insertions to accommodate him fully. I soon found I could take all of him inside me. I rolled my pelvis onto him and then arched my back, pulling out. He kissed and enjoyed my soapy tits in his face. I playfully shimmied side to side, back and forth, gently slapping his handsome face with my budding boobs.

The sensation was amazing, even in the limited space of the bathtub. I began humping him with a faster cadence, and it didn't take long before he started breathing heavily and moaning. I sensed that my humping motions were pleasing to him, but what it really meant was that he was about to fire his torpedoes into my submarine pen. Before I knew what was happening, he gripped me by my hips and convulsed as he deposited his seed into my love cave.

Not really understanding the mechanics of the human penis, I grabbed ahold of it and replaced it at the entrance for another shagging. I had not climaxed yet and wanted to feel that delicious bone inside me. Beckley, on the other hand, wanted to get out of the tub. Even though I didn't quite climax, playing submarine pens was the most erotic experience of my life. I had earned my water wings. Now he needed time to recharge. I suspected this new thing between us was going to become an addiction.

Private showings

Private parties

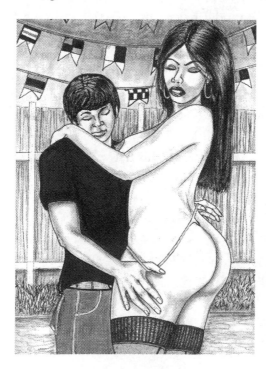

After that experience in the bathtub, Beckley wasn't just Beckley anymore. He was my guy now. I hadn't expected to be in this situation. He seemed so mature and wise for a young man. We explored each other's bodies and tried various different positions. Beckley had a vast porn collection, and we watched videos so I could learn how to perform oral sex. I thought it was fascinating, and he returned the favor whenever we could find a private place. We saw each other exclusively every day after that. I was fast becoming his personal groupie. He taught me quite a few things in the bedroom, and we were careful to use condoms. Unfortunately, Mom was emptying out the trash from my room one day and discovered them. She gave me a scolding and warned me not to "give it up," all the while fully knowing that Pandora's Box was already opened.

In the weeks that followed, Beckley increased his dominance over me. I passively cooperated and encouraged him to take me in hand. Beckley directed me to come down to his flat each day to play sex games. He tied me spread-eagle to his bed, shaved my pubic area smooth, and gave me small tricks to perform. I learned to play fetch with his underwear, cleaned his room, and completed household chores while he enjoyed watching and groping me. Each day, he would conjure up some new task or game he wanted me to perform. He never ran out of ideas.

As the weeks passed by, one thing led to another. He dictated what he wanted me to do, and I felt compelled and happy to comply. It was risky but sensual and gratifying. He knew how to push my buttons and make me do things I normally wouldn't. I developed into a skilled fellatrix. I found it stimulating and prided myself on being able to follow his oral protocol.

After his mother left in the morning, he called me to down to his apartment wearing next to nothing. Sometimes I only wore a bra and panties, was topless, or wore only a large T-shirt and heels. I loved the adrenaline kick it gave me when I opened my door and started my chancy trek to his flat without being seen by someone in the building. Sometimes he made me wait outside his door and beg him, sing a song, or memorize some silly password in order to be let inside. Some days, he would just hold and kiss me, undressed as I was, in the hallway with the door wide open.

How on earth did he know how these things turned me on? I loved his style and found him to be an incredibly sexy beast of a man-boy! His attitude was completely off the charts, and his confidence bordered on being arrogant. When he gave me directions, I paid attention. With a hand signal, I knew when it was time to get on my knees.

We took risks. He would pull up my skirt or pull my jeans down and harpoon me in the laundry room, in the stairwell, on the roof, in the basement, and once in the hallway. His favorite thing was a quick oral session in the elevator. We came very close to being caught on one occasion.

He trained me to do more risqué practices, like holding his spend in my mouth, gargling, or swishing it around and then opening wide so he could see just the gooey pool before I swallowed. It was just a matter of time before we got into trouble; yet this fact didn't stop us. It was like an itch that had to be scratched.

After all the years growing up, I suppose when one attains a certain age, something can trigger a game-changing emotional event such as this one. I was just weeks away from my seventeenth birthday when my third awakening experience with Beckley occurred. He didn't need to issue any threats; he acted as if he fully expected me to do his bidding without question.

Preparing her for a deep cleansing

Domestic chores in my uniform

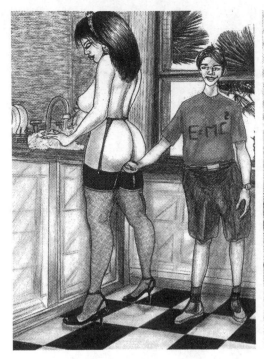

Groped                                    Domestic service

On one occasion, I fell short of his expectations. We were at Washington Square on a Friday evening. People were playing music, roller skating, and milling about. I was adorned in glow jewelry. He asked me to tie his shoelace for him while we were chatting with some friends. I refused. He slapped me harshly across my bottom side and repeated his demand. I didn't say anything, but my eyes brimmed with tears.

The real reason I was so near to sobbing in public was not because I was hurt, but because I felt awful for letting him down and refusing to tie his shoe. I never wanted to disappoint him. He instilled that in me. It didn't matter that we were among other people who were surprised by the swat on my butt. I wiped my tears away, smiled, and then got down on my knees and tied his shoelace.

I became obsessed with him and the naughty things we did together. Groping, fondling, or smooching at a bus stop or while on the number 5 or 6 train was not unusual for us.

Beckley took advantage of me, and I liked the clever way he did it. From the moment he audaciously grabbed my nipples through my clothes and kissed me, I was *his.* How he became so advanced sexually, I will never know. My guess is that he found his divorced father's porn collection or had studied it on the newfangled invention, the Internet. After all, there are always easily accessible oceans of smut.

I developed a growing anticipation for the little games he invented for us to play. I was his favorite student, and he was my teacher. What I didn't realize was that a lot of the local homeboys coveted me secretly. Beckley wanted it known that I was his girl. It brought him a certain elevated status among the other guys. I saw the change in his friends, but it just didn't register that it was because of me. I didn't have a solid self-concept yet.

I was the girl who couldn't say no. I was now Beckley's girl, and when we attended social get-togethers, we always played it up just to let everyone know of the good thing we had going.

Scrubbing the patio

Cheesecake on demand

Challenging tasks

During inclement weather, I would end up topless or totally undressed the entire day. Beckley loved watching me do domestic chores in the raw. He also played Hollywood director, and I played the part of his leading actress. While washing dishes, tidying up his room, or doing whatever needed to be done, he liked me to be dressed in my birthday suit. Mind you, we still had to get the chores done before his mother came home. We were careful to hide the evidence of our sexual adventures. I was genuinely in love and getting *some* on a regular basis, if you know what I mean. I completely ignored the voice inside telling me I was throwing caution to the wind and growing up too fast.

When you love someone, the darker side of them doesn't look as dark. This young man dominated me so exquisitely. The more challenging or perplexing the tasks he made up for me, the more sexually stimulated I became. He taught me how he desired for me to use my body to please him.

Being an airy Libran, I liked to skim the surface and keep things breezy and fun. Beckley was just the opposite. He was a stickler for details. It was like a political decision for him. A simple oral worship session was regimented down to a strict protocol. He gave me plenty of practice, too.

He trained me how to perform and satisfy him, and I believe it was Beckley who set a new course for my life. I learned how to do "it" very well. It became a skill that he would help me perfect. I would practice it for the next decade and beyond. It became my livelihood for many years.

Striptease shows                    The audition at the cabaret

It wasn't long after I was seduced (make that, tamed and trained) that Beckley had monopolized my time. I dressed sexier, changed my hairstyle, refreshed my makeup periodically (every fifteen minutes, whether I needed it or not), and generally acted as window dressing when we went out. Beckley insisted that I always look my best. He picked out the cosmetics I was to use liberally on my pretty face, and I donned articles from my new, sexy wardrobe whenever we went out. I should have been disturbed by this. Instead, I felt free and alive. I was special when I was with him. I did not feel restricted at all, even though he held me on a short leash.

Each day, he had a new trick for me to learn. I was organically transformed into his test subject. I was enthusiastic about being the most cooperative star pupil of his sexual tutelage. He was conditioning me to learn the basics of submissive pet play, and I learned my lessons very well. He was the instructor, and I was the student. I learned to crawl on all fours on a leash, roll over, and beg, just like a pet. I passively encourage it; I wanted to serve. It made me tingle. He led me onto riskier behaviors, and I welcomed them. I soon found myself watching video clips, learning how to do exotic striptease routines and submissive pet play. It was my job to learn new tricks. Ironically, my biggest fear was losing him, not that I was becoming a submissive pet slave.

The first time I exposed my body for other guys was at a party in the East Village. We attended a pay-per-view title fight and birthday party. The host and birthday boy was a balding older gentleman in a wheelchair. He was a friend of Beckley's father. His name was Hector, and he was Beckley's informal mentor and godfather. I discovered later he was a retired public servant living off a good pension.

A mixed crowd was there. Age groups varied, and there were no racial barriers either. I didn't really know any of the guests. That evening, Beckley dressed me in a form-fitting yellow summer mini-dress with matching four-inch heels. That was all. There was plenty of beer, shish-kabobs, and grilled chicken.

I was amazed how well Hector got around on those wheels. I sat in a crowd of people, watching the fights. Looking around the room, I noticed there were five or six guys playing poker with Beckley at the table in the kitchen. Some others played dominoes near the utility room, and a larger group (about thirty of us) tightly squeezed into folding chairs, watching the fight.

During the second round, Beckley called me out of my seat, and I walked over to the card table. As I stood next to him, he brazenly slipped his hand up my dress from behind, touching my nether zone. I didn't say anything or even flinch. I didn't look at anyone's face, either. I wanted desperately to see if anyone else was watching me being felt up, but I couldn't quite bring myself to do it. I lit his smoke as calmly as I could with a small disposable lighter from my hand purse. "Thanks, babe!" he said, and with that, he removed his hand from my dirty bits and swatted my butt smartly enough to goose me on my way. That was yet another proverbial "good girl" gesture, wasn't it?

Beckley's actions brought a few chuckles from the guys at the table. I could sense the hushed admiration he received from his young fellow card players for having a hot girl to run his hands over while his smoke was lit for him. Even though it was degrading, I actually felt a measure of pride in this small task. Beckley's stock was rising with the fellas because he possessed a *hottie* like me.

After the fight, most folks had already left. Beckley hung back and was deep in conversation with Hector. The living room was empty except for the multitude of extra foldable chairs. Might as well make myself useful, eh? While Beckley continued his conversation, I removed and stacked the chairs in the converted garage that was now just a storage area with a ramp for Hector's motorized wheelchair. After all the chairs were stowed, I went to Beckley and sat down by his side.

Cocktail waitress at the cabaret

"Can't you see the men are talking?" Beckley growled in an exaggerated New York accent. I was startled by this remark and backed away. Hector called out that I should stay and listen to his idea. He wheeled himself into the garage while we followed. He explained how everything could be arranged to make room for a small platform. It didn't dawn on me that they were setting up a main stage for an upcoming bachelor party. I was to dance naked at the upcoming party!

Hector and Beckley assigned me to serve as an exotic dancer at Hector's nephew's bachelor party. I was going to be the entertainment. When I realized the deal they were making, I suddenly felt like I had bitten off more than I could chew. I wasn't too sure I was ready to expose my naked body on stage in front of strange men. I could privately strip for Beckley, but not in front of a crowd under the effects of alcohol. That was a pretty tall order! I was going to refuse regardless of the consequences. It was non-negotiable. But that wasn't all. Beckley also promised Hector I would flash him my goodies as a personal birthday present.

Beckley pointed to the spot on the cement floor. "Stand here, turn around, bend over, spread your legs, and then use both hands to open yourself," he ordered matter-of-factly. I froze and stood there like confused robot.

Beckley then said something to the effect of, "She's not too smart. I apologize for that, Hector. Come here! Let me help you, Tessa!" He roughly turned me away from Hector and pushed the small of my back until I bent at the waist. He lifted up the hem of my dress, draped it over my shoulders, and used his hands to open my cheeks wide. I felt totally embarrassed and ashamed by being put on display for this man.

Hector whistled and high-fived Beckley, shouting out, "Fine pedigree, Morris! I think she will do just fine!" I was informed that I had one week to learn the script and practice my technique for the bachelor party.

The next Friday evening, I arrived wearing my royal red robe, and as I entered the party, sensual music started. I slowly strolled in step with the music up to the makeshift stage and dropped the robe to the floor, kicking it off to the smiling Beckley. He gave me a wink of encouragement. I instantly felt better about being at the all-male party.

There I stood in my turquoise sequined bra and bikini bottom and brand-new five-inch platform stilettos. About twenty approving gentlemen were present. All eyes were on me as the lights dimmed slightly over the audience and were made brighter on me. Beckley passed the chair up to me, and I set it center stage. The lucky bachelor was cajoled and prodded up on stage. I dropped to my knees in front of him, bringing temporary pandemonium from the audience. I unzipped him and pulled down his pants below his knees. I told him to bend over and hold the chair while facing away from the audience. I removed his thin leather dress belt from his pants and stood to the side while he actually assumed the position for me. Hector shouted out that he needed a good spanking for hanging out with a stripper the night before he was getting married.

I gave him ten dramatic strokes across his behind, right through his briefs. I gave him a couple of nice hard whacks, too. The audience counted them in a chanting fashion. It was all in good fun, and soon we had him sitting in the chair with his hands handcuffed behind him. It was now time for the whipped cream and the lap dance. I writhed and rubbed myself all over him. Removing my bra, I let him place his face in my cleavage. I sprayed whipped cream on my breasts, and he licked it off, to the delight of everyone. I placed lipstick kiss marks all over his collar, neck, and face while camera flashes erupted all round us.

After the bachelor was fully processed, a few other audience members came up for lap dances as well. I had a fine sheen of sweat on my skin as I ground my hips on the fourteenth and final patron.

After the stage show, I placed my bra back on and served drinks and snacks to the guys, who generously put singles and fives in my waistband. I had $221 in my purse just from tips. I received another $85 (a fifty-fifty split this time) when I put my robe back on to leave that evening. It was a whole new ballgame.

One month later, I was putting on sexy shows for other private parties. I put on simple and elaborate shows on stairways, in garages, on rooftops, in basements, in storage rooms, on back patios, or in empty apartments. These all became my stages where I performed.

Beckley took me downtown once to an empty building. We bought a slice and took the freight elevator to an abandoned seventh-floor corner office. We smoked and enjoyed the view of the sea of humanity blanketing the walkways of midtown. He then lifted my skirt, pulled my panties down to my knees, and rammed me from behind right in front of an open window. I watched the people below as they walked by. All the while, Beckley repeatedly porked me from behind. It was surreal but wonderfully fulfilling. To be screwed like that in an open window was a potent and thrilling experience. It always was when I was with Beckley.

The window was open, and the sun was warm. It was a fantastic feeling. I felt like this was a special moment, a pledge of his love for me. I truly loved Beckley. He was on my wavelength. No one on the street seemed to notice or care that I was being boffed from behind in the window. A few pedestrians looked up, saw me hanging slightly out of the window, and then went about their business, totally unaware. His man-juice leaked out of me all the way home.

Cleaning the rims of Beckley's BMW

Beckley and I were making money working parties and putting on shows. The stairwell at his new place in Yonkers was my next proving ground. The staircase leading down to the basement was a favorite place to put on shows. I shimmied, jiggled, and stripped down for the entertainment of an all-male audience. I was paid to dance and showcase my naked charms. Beckley taught me specific routines. I was instructed how to move my hips and wriggle to elicit a lustful response like the professionals. I practiced dancing different steps to broaden my marketability. I didn't realize it at the time, but I was learning skills that would serve me well years later. He wanted me to move my body just as he choreographed. He contended that it would elicit the desired effect from an all-male audience.

Beckley and I were inseparable. Beckley became my fulltime lover and professional trainer. I always felt safe, knowing that he was nearby to protect me. He knew what he wanted me to do and molded me.

I felt I was in my element, and even though he could be strict with me, I realized he had a good heart and wanted me to be the best I could be. There was still a nagging feeling that what I was doing would someday backfire on me. I tried not to think about negative consequences of my actions but rationalized them.

I was just like my mother. And just like my mother, I was occasionally hand-spanked smartly as foreplay or correction. I accepted it. My corrective therapy sessions became more ritualized. At first, I was mildly appalled by Beckley's use of corporal punishment. How dare he strike my bottom like that? I soon learned to just accept it as part of our sexual practice and conditioning regimen. He may have placed a few welts or red marks on my bottom side, but he never harmed me. I trusted Beckley.

I am a totally right-brained person, so I reasoned that I had to practice daily and improve as a dancer or performer. I could understand that. After all, he had worked so hard to arrange the showings for paying customers; the least I could do was put on a good performance. If it meant getting a few bites from that whippy little cane or belt to focus me, so be it. I guess I still needed a nudge now and then to understand my role. Beckley was happy with our new secret enterprise, and I was happy that he was pleased.

Whenever going out, I was meticulously dressed. Every occasion was a public event for Beckley. It was merely business—clingy, abbreviated mini-dresses and heels for me. Some of the outfits he insisted on were, shall we say, eye-catching. I towered over him by a good four or five inches (especially in my heels), and he seemed to get a strange charge out of the height difference. Beckley thought of himself as a tamer of an Amazon woman or something in that realm of male conquest. That six-inch little man in his pants was my trophy. It was like the comic book I had found years earlier—the superheroine being tamed by a small, calculating man. When in public, he liked me to always be dressed in appearance-enhancing garb. Other guys took notice.

I was usually his silent, sexy companion. He didn't like me to speak, so he would put a golf ball or glass marble in my mouth. When we went out or partied with other guys, I smiled a lot, giggled, grunted, mewled, and moaned but didn't talk much. I was to be seen, admired, and ogled, and my job was to fawn all over Beckley. That was about it. I lit his smokes, tied his shoes, took his coat, buffed his nails, poured his drinks, and did errands for him.

Other guys saw me as Beckley's sexy personal valet. I didn't know it at the time, but Beckley was gradually turning me out, and he slowly evolved from being my lover to behaving more like a pimp. I admit I am not the sharpest tool in the shed, and I found it simpler to just follow Beckley's lead.

I was groomed smooth from my neckline on down, and my clitoris and tongue were pierced. So under his spell was I that I offered my backside for a tattoo, but he refused. Beckley contended that he already owned it, so why did he have to mark it up? It sounded right to me, and besides, tattoos were painful, expensive, and permanent.

Our sexual exploits started out just between the two of us, but after a while, we progressed to private shows and parties. Displaying my breasts, dipping my nipples in a guy's drink, and personalizing my panties using a sharpie marker (with an autograph and date) for tips were just a few simple tasks I learned to do.

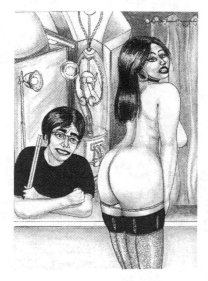

Vantessa in training

Taking direction

As my training and development progressed, I was used as a human vase. I was positioned naked, lying flat on my back, and a glass tube inserted into my upturned vagina with a spray of flowers placed inside the tube. My knees were pulled back to my ears, and I was made to hold that pose for a good fifteen minutes. I was a human decorative conversation piece. I was also taken to a party where the client wanted a special showing. I was given a makeover beforehand, as the client was paying a premium price for what I was about to do.

For another special private party that I worked, I was instructed to wear black-seamed stockings with a matching lace garter belt, six-inch heels, and a collar and leash. My hair was tied schoolgirl-style, and my face was made up to look like a sexy feline woman. I actually felt catlike as I prepared to make my entrance. At the appointed time, the back door was opened, and I crawled in, joining the unsuspecting patrons.

I totally mesmerized the all-male crowd. They were silent as I meowed and sensually rubbed up against the pant legs of the guests. I dramatically slinked and purred as I strutted on all fours. Catcalls galore were thrown in my direction. After making one complete circuit through the party space, I awaited the signal to proceed with my next task. I had prepared for it and was aching to get it over with.

Outside on the patio was a small plastic toddler's pool filled with kitty litter. At the appointed time, I crawled on all fours into the tiny pool of cat litter like the feline I was playing. I scratched around a bit, wagged the kitty tail inside my naked bottom, squatted, and then facing my audience, urinated into the cat litter-filled pool. It splashed noisily; I couldn't believe it was happening. Would it ever end? It seemed to keep rushing out with no sign of stopping. The crowd howled and whistled their approval with cheers, applause, and several calls of, "Here, kitty-kitty! Good pussycat!"

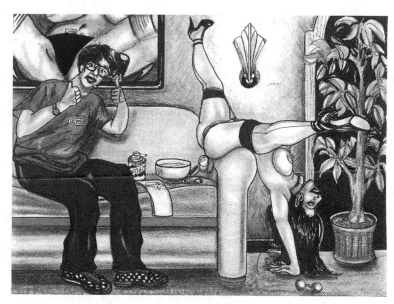

Grooming—no hair below the neck

After spurting three more times to finish my spectacle, the seemingly twelve-minute urination session was over. I was just glad I was able to quickly let the bursting torrent out of my bladder. I had downed six glasses of water beforehand so I would be able to easily let it out. I would never have been able to relax and just pee in front of a complete group of male partygoers ogling me in a very intimate moment. Now what? I was just stuck inside that wet kitty litter. Climbing out was somehow more challenging than climbing inside. After my presentation, I was paid $500 cash. I thanked the client and also chatted for a bit with my new fans. I excused myself before I started drinking and thought of giving private extra shows. I put my trench coat on right over my scanty cat costume and left for home. The ride back that late at night was a bit more intense.

It was over-the-top, but I wasn't emotionally distraught by my new occupation. Beckley told me to look at it like it was just a job. How far would this relationship go before it self-destructed? In the back of my mind, I knew this couldn't last forever. I knew I couldn't keep this up. I was doing things that were not entirely moral or legal, and it would only be a matter of time before the rug would be pulled out from under me. Instead of taking counsel from my dear mother, I was listening to this eighteen-year-old boy—not the wisest move I ever made.

I had already been with Beckley for several months when I obtained an expensive but well-made false ID saying I was twenty-one. I dropped out of school and began cocktailing and dancing at two different men's clubs downtown. The money that I earned was so good that we were able to upgrade our living space. I gave most of the money to him. Beckley was good with money. He saved, allotted, budgeted, and still had some left over to buy fashionable clothes and accessories for me. I was even given an allowance.

Together, we were able to find a nicer refurbished basement apartment away from the watchful eyes of our mothers (bless their hearts). It was there that we set up a private entertainment room. The empty room served as our playroom, and Beckley even had a stripper pole installed. This room was our very own place where I could learn new moves. The more I practiced my dancing, the more skills I developed. We were riding the wave.

It never occurred to me that the psychological investment and sacrifices I had made by choosing to live like a sexy bimbo robot would soon come to an end. I had to grow up sometime, didn't I? I pushed these thoughts to the back of my mind and concentrated on my dancing.

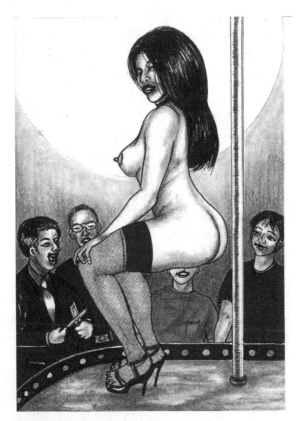

# The Stairway (Twelve Steps): Confession #4

It was a cheesy setup, but it had its merits. I shall never forget those twelve wooden basement stairs. A mirror ball, blacklight, portable multicolor light module spraying out low-intensity laser beams, and rows of six to a dozen chairs at the bottom landing made up my private makeshift theater.

Each time, I made my entrance the same way, using the twelve-step signature routine to get the party started. Beckley and I studied instructional stripper videos and cherry-picked the moves we liked. He incorporated them into a striptease show. I practiced them intently, trying to emulate the moves perfectly. My problem was a tendency to watch myself in the mirror as I danced and moved. My narcissistic tendency has never left me. I received smart strokes of the whippy cane a few times during rehearsal. I resented it at times, too. I was eighteen years old, and although Beckley was also eighteen, his connections with Hector and other friends of his estranged father enabled us to continue with business.

I admit there were times when I considered cutting and running. I was old enough to do what I wanted. On a few occasions, I entertained thoughts of going out on my own. I still loved him, but I needed my own space. The space between us was growing.

Beckley used an electronic keyboard and amplifier to create a repeating loop of beats that I can still hear in the back of my mind to this day. It had a long, four-measure sound and accompanying electronic harmonies, and it actually sounded pretty good.

Beckley also fancied himself a promoter and director. He had carefully choreographed a dance routine for me. He had exact steps and actions in mind, and he applied that thin bamboo cane to my ass or legs on more than one occasion—not enough to hurt, but it certainly got my complete attention. I learned my steps. That was the juice, along with the fact I was making those boys at the bottom of the stairs lust after me.

A saucy, sensual tune started and cued me to begin my strut. When Beckley flicked the whippy cane on my butt, I knew it was my time to start. It was his way of prompting me to go through my paces. His attention to detail taught me that every dance move I make is important. Practicing every day, I learned my steps down cold. I was so proud when I gave private performances for Beckley and his guests. The men whistled and clapped at my precision. Tips were abundant.

I found Beckley to be a good talker and a sharp businessman. Growing up a poor white boy in New York taught him to use his God-given skills. He had the gift of gab. He would occasionally invite a few of his friends over and then say, "Hey, fellas, you have to see Tessa's new routine!"

No clothes? No problem.

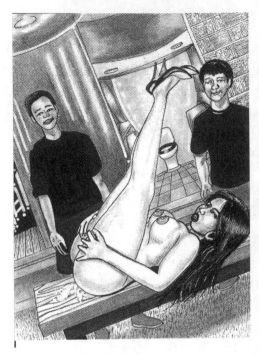 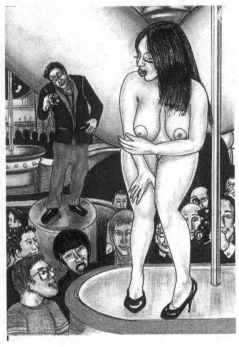

Grooming inspection                    Dancing at the Platinum Club

Without the lights, bells, and whistles, I would perform rehearsal in jeans and a pullover. Beckley's music started to play. (He was proud of his music.) I enacted the exact movements to the music, fully dressed. It should also be noted that I like being nude. Clothes are so confining. My skin needs to breathe. It is a challenge to be a nudist in the age of big brother, especially in a city as large and intrusive as New York. It can be done, though.

The fully clothed rehearsal for his friends was a great way to entice them to come back for the real show, and he reminded them to bring their wallets. The gentlemen who observed my twelve-step show rehearsal were appreciative of my moves, and the entire routine was popular. To see me jiggle and wiggle my way down the stairs—butt first, no less—whet their appetites.

The promise of me repeating the process wearing only a tiny costume was an irresistible attraction for them. Beckley preferred me to wear the Day-Glo one-piece romper as I descended the steps—no brag, just fact. The personal eye contact I gave to each of them as I worked my way to the bottom of the stairs was a tempting draw. Wearing next to nothing in a pseudo-nightclub atmosphere, we put on a special presentation. Primitive though it was, six of the twelve chairs arranged in a semicircle always had paying customers. They howled, whistled, and yelled, *"Mira, mira, mira!"* as I worked my way down.

It was a brilliant yet simple thing, just strutting down a set of twelve stairs wearing a tiny bra and thong or a romper, wiggling, jiggling, and all the while licking a phallic-shaped lollipop.

Nursing

Greetings!

I can still hear that series of beats in my head today. The music started, and I had to strut (on cue) into view from the top of the landing. I wore a lime green or blazing orange romper glowing under the blacklight, and it was showtime. The romper was a silky-smooth, single piece of stretching material that ran through my legs and up inside my butt crack, flaring up on either side of my back and over my shoulders, with just enough sheer material to cover most of my nipple caps before joining the piece once again covering my baby-smooth pubic area.

On the top landing, wearing a blaze-orange romper and five-inch heels, I strutted three steps forward, pivoted like a soldier, turned, and faced my audience from the upper landing. The clients sat at the bottom of the stairway, quiet at first. The lighting effects were amateur at best but a nice distraction from the primitive setting. Due to the lighting, it was difficult to see my audience until I got halfway down the stairs.

The gentlemen of the audience were generally friends of Hector or Beckley. They were both blue- and white-collar young men in their twenties to mid-forties.

I had to remember my musical cues, and at just the right instant, pull the romper away, exposing my breasts. Then I covered them again with a wink and a smile—a tease of what was yet to come. I would lick my lollipop dramatically and then begin my next set of moves. I strutted in place like a marching soldier until the music cued me to begin my downward stepping routine. I looked at the faces sitting in their chairs; all eyes were on me. I felt a sense of pride and newfound self-worth. I was the center of attention. I was a star.

I paused, teased, turned, and then licked my lime green lollipop just for effect before I descended the stairs. I concentrated on my moves, hoping I wouldn't tumble in my five-inch mules on those rickety wooden slats.

I held the rail and high-stepped my way down the first three steps. Then, on perfect cue, I completely turned around and swished my way slowly down the next three steps backward, showing my bottom cheeks to the audience. I bounced and gyrated just like the girls in X-rated videos.

The guys watching me were quite appreciative. They whistled and yelled as I rolled the thin material away from my butt crack and did an exaggerated shimmy down to step number nine.

Without missing a beat, I swayed and writhed like a harem girl trying to beguile and seduce her sheik. At the right chord, I let go of the railing and carefully reached down, holding the bottom step and then looking back to spread my legs wider for the enthusiastic audience. I was met with cheers and gasps of excitement. I looked between my legs at the guys, who were amazed and excited by my wanton display. I licked my lollipop, winked, and smiled for effect. I realized a surge of power and accomplishment. I felt sexy, like an adored Egyptian princess. I watched their eyes soaking up all of me.

I moved backward to the music down the last three steps to the chairs. I saw the effect it had on my audience—tent poles in their trousers and all eyes on my barely-covered buns. They were fascinated with my feminine assets and reaching for their wallets as I got closer.

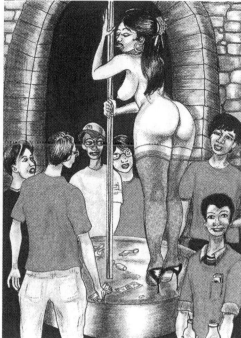

Shaking her cans                    Entertaining Beckley's guests

Once on the concrete basement floor with its chipped red paint, I did a slow pole dance using one of the support beams. I shook and bobbed my rump, bounced my boobs, and undulated to the suggestive musical beats. The guys loved it when I made love to the support beam. I teased and taunted them mercilessly. On Beckley's signal, I gave special attention to the clients who paid extra for some personal contact or a special lap dance.

I received tips for doing the extra lap dances and private grope dances behind a curtain (just a blanket hanging over a clothesline). Beckley collected the money for us. He kept about 65 percent because, as he explained, he had to do most of the work; all I really had to do was dance and shake my ass for a bit. At first, it sounded reasonable, because at the time, I had no head for business. After all, he had to contact and arrange clients to see me put on a show, right? Still, the boys came to see me, not him! This troubled me. The problem that I didn't want to acknowledge at the time was that our dom-and-sub relationship was transforming into a purely business relationship. He was less interested in me as a lover and more into the business aspect.

When not working parties or private showings, I found myself, four times each week, rushing to board the train to get downtown. I worked at three different men's clubs. I sometimes worked double shifts for days at a time. This lifestyle was no longer working for me, and I began to ask myself what exactly I was getting out of it. I grew tired of the constant boredom of the adult industry. Was I becoming jaded? I feared that I was being changed and possibly headed for a ruinous end. And I wasn't quite nineteen yet.

On a brighter side, I met all kinds of people while cocktailing or dancing. Men from every walk of life came to see me dance or serve drinks. Many of the men who slipped dollars into my waistband were from out of town. Some gave me generous tips and promised a lot of things. It wasn't hard work, and I learned quite a bit about how businesses like this are run.

Nipple modification

Cheerful serving girl

I learned that at least 50 percent of the girls in the exotic dance profession are bisexual or gay. I became sexually turned on 25–50 percent of the time while working my shift. The amount of money I made varied. Some nights, I took home much less than $100, and some evenings, I took home $1,400 or more.

I learned about the in-house politics of working as a dancer in a men's club. I am basically a positive and friendly person, and I like to stay on good terms with people. I do not dance like the other girls. It was mostly due to me, not my dance training. I use my hands to express my inner dancer. Most girls wrap themselves around the pole or make crude gestures with their butts in archaic, stereotypical fashion. Ironically, it seems guys never tire of that primitive dance method.

My personal style hasn't negatively affected me. Dancing can be highly political. I stayed out of the political arena, avoided skirmishes with the resident hateful bitches, and watched the drama queens do their thing from behind the scenes. If the manager needed a dancer on short notice, they could usually count on me to show up on a day off or work a double shift. I never became close to the bouncers. As a result, I was considered an outsider, albeit a reliable one.

The money was flowing in, and it wasn't really that hard of a job. I found that if I could entertain the clients while putting up with the extremely cold air conditioning, smoky stale air, makeshift dressing rooms, rude patrons, and blaring loud music, that it wasn't so bad being naked in front of strangers. I got used to it.

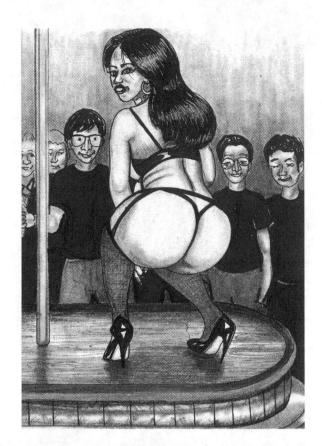

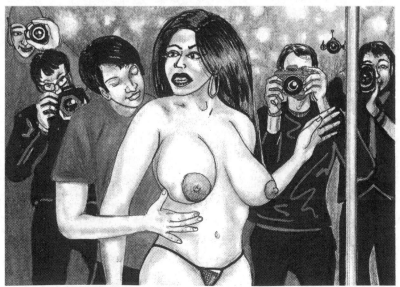

# Next Level: Confession #5

After saving a small fortune, Beckley took me out to buy new toys and clothes. We were living together and felt like a married couple. He bought some nice suits for himself and sexy leisure wear for me. We were in good standing with the local erotic boutique stores. Beckley paid cash for a small New York Special preowned BMW from a friend in Queens. It wasn't perfect, but it had low miles and was mechanically sound.

It was only because of my earning power that Beckley was able to buy the car for a single cash payment. He shared how he was going to pimp his new ride out on the way home. It was then that I realized he had taken me out to buy some nice things just to placate me while he bought himself the BMW 3 series.

In public, I was always dressed like a sexy girl going to a cocktail party. My growing collection of stylish Italian heels made my mother suspicious. The look suited me, as long as Beckley was happy. I had to look perfect whenever Beckley took me out in public. He had pictures of different ensembles he wanted me to wear. The Bettie Page look was one of his favorites and came complete with a Cleopatra wig.

I was getting burned out working as a cocktail waitress and dancer at multiple men's clubs. At the same time, I had never been more successful. Out of synch with reality (per usual for me), I was gaining popularity with the downtown adult entertainment club owners.

 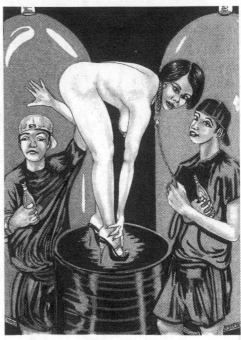

She's over here, fellas!

My very first completely nude table dance was for an internationally mixed group of men. It was my first night at that particular club, and it was quite a wakeup call. They wanted me to spread myself open so they could see my dirty bits. At $40 a dance, I danced for four sets. The club had five stages in rotation (one main stage and four smaller satellite stages). Each rotation required three songs each on the main stage and then moving to the next smaller stage in succession. The entire rotation took ten to twelve minutes per stage multiplied by five stages, taking nearly an hour to complete. Then it was time to refresh, circulate the floor, meet the clients, and provide table or lap dances.

At the end of the night, my feet hurt, and I smelled of stale body spray, wine, and tobacco smoke. I was ready to hang up the thong and heels for a while. Beckley wouldn't hear of it. He lectured, cajoled, and coerced me into going back night after night until I wasn't just burned out, but also worn out. I didn't care as much about pleasing Beckley or my patrons anymore. My dance routines became more mechanical. I was merely going through the motions. I wanted a break, a vacation, time off. I was barely nineteen years of age and needed some "me" time. It wasn't to be for a while.

I had been dancing for nearly a year already, and I ended up ultimately pole-dancing and stripping on stages coast-to-coast for more than thirteen years following my first time shimmying out on the main stage. I danced at large, well-appointed, established clubs and small, one-stage, broken-down sleaze joints as well. I learned that it is the contact between the dancers and the clients that matters most; the other stuff, even the tips and compensation, are just hygiene factors.

I was earning from fairly decent to better-than-average money, and even though mom was suspicious of where I might be getting it at times, she enjoyed the fact that I was helping pay the bills each month. By this time, she had accepted a job at a security guard service in midtown. We both worked mainly nights. I bought her some nice things, dinner out each week, and some jewelry. Mom's weakness is jewelry. To this very day, she gets an adrenaline rush when she goes to a jewelry store—and Canal Street has several square blocks of them.

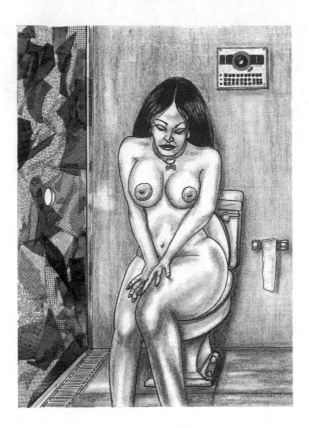

One day, over cheesecake and a cup of coffee at her favorite café, I opened up. I spilled the beans with Mom and told her everything. When I explained to her that I had dropped out of school in my junior year to become a dancer, she acted like I had slapped her. My dear mother explained that she had also, in her younger days, been an exotic dancer in Miami and Puerto Rico. That is how she met my father, rest his soul. She gradually discovered that I was dancing and cocktailing but didn't stop me or even acknowledge that she knew about it. She told me she hoped for better things for me than to be an exotic dancer. Suddenly, I felt like an underachiever. I had failed my mother.

Beckley and I moved again, into a small apartment in Washington Heights, and I could see Yankee Stadium all lit at night from our room. Beckley bought a cage for me. It had a nice, soft rubber mat and was just large enough to accommodate me. He also purchased some attachments to allow for toy and vibe insertions while inside. One of the things I had loved about Beckley was how he could turn any situation, no matter where we were or what we were doing, into a sexually stimulating adventure for me. For my part, I prided myself in being spontaneously submissive. The new pet play training put passion back into our relationship again, at least temporarily.

It was not unusual for Beckley to walk me to the corner store by a leash connected to a cheap-looking dog collar. People stared at us and laughed, but I was only too proud to be a pet for Beckley, my owner and master. Oh, yes! It bothered me at first, but after a while, I just grinned when people looked at me strangely. I always felt like Beckley was testing and training me, and I wanted to be the best pet for him. I adopted the mindset he instilled in me. I craved his love and approval.

Little did I know that he had received everything from me except what he really and truly wanted. Strangely enough, Beckley wanted to impregnate me in the worst way. He wanted my stomach round and bulging out. It would be his supreme achievement—Vantessa as his baby mama!

Feeling like a failure

Hearing the sound of her master's voice

I had no idea of the accolades and respect he received from his friends and brothers in the hood. He was a celebrity now. I hadn't realized before that I had been lusted after by mostly all of the red-blooded heterosexual males in the neighborhood. How was I to know? Making me a baby mama would have been his crowning achievement. I was now a certified hot girl in the hood. I had achieved something special on my own social level—my fifteen minutes, right? Beckley was getting what every guy in our neighborhood and their brothers and fathers wanted: me!

That was true until I overheard someone mention in passing to another guy that Beckley had plans for me. Little by little, I realized Beckley might be planning to put me out on the streets or sell me to a street pimp. He was going to put me up for sale! How could he possibly do that? I had noticed that he was not as interested in making love to me as he used to be. I had even performed extra-special events for his friends and given sexual favors to pay some of his debts or for a bag of weed. Life turns on a dime, doesn't it? One week, we were in our new apartment in Washington Heights with a brand-new pet cage and regimen, and the next thing I knew, the proverbial pilot light was burned out.

I loved Beckley and thrilled at the things he made me do, but I did not want to become a street whore. Once a girl is led down that path, it is damn hard to escape. I could see the girls out walking the street, at 4:00 or 5:00 a.m., always looking for the next John. It was dangerous work. I watched one such working girl being disciplined by her pimp in an alley with jumper cables. I encountered it just about every night leaving the club at closing. It is an unhealthy profession and a temporary one for most girls, who either end up dead, in jail, or hapless junkies. I imagined some of those ladies of the evening were once young hotties, like me, on their way up the adult sex industry ladder. Was this the final outcome for girls like me? The thought pained me.

Is the real Vantessa revealing herself?

In the coming weeks, Beckley seemed less inclined to touch me. The thrill was gone. It was like a roller coaster of emotions now—sometimes up, sometimes way down. No matter how he screwed me, I never got pregnant. He tried everything to breed me. By now, our sexual encounters were reduced to up-the-skirt quickies. It was over. Both of us were bored.

They say familiarity breeds contempt, and that is exactly what happened with Beckley and me. After the novelty wore off, he hardly ever touched me, instead keeping me increasingly engaged in work while he went out with friends or went to lay some beats down at a local recording studio. He fancied himself a lover, a fighter, and a vanilla hip-hop G.

My greatest fear had been losing him. I had given everything to him, against Mom's better judgment. Now he seemed bored with me. I was being left alone on my own with greater frequency with each passing week. I saw the lights from Yankee Stadium and wondered if he was there with someone else.

In the middle of the night, he would come home, flip on the lights, and wake me out of a sound sleep to bake a frozen dinner or pizza rolls or go on a run for snacks. Then I had to serve drinks to his friends while they played video games. I always did my best to be cheerful and cooperative, but there were times when I rebelled. I could see the curiosity and wonderment in the eyes of his friends. How could a sloppy blonde white kid like Beckley make at hot chick like me to do all this for him?

This didn't happen very often, as I worked most nights until 4:00 or 5:00 a.m. I usually arrived home just before sunrise.

Beckley then started to leave me for a few days at a time or for a weekend in Connecticut. He claimed he was with his mom, but I found that he lied about that. He was nice enough to put in a designated friend as a companion so I wasn't alone all of the time. The surrogate, a close friend of his, was there, enjoying himself, maybe even being paid, to make sure I made it to work. His surrogates even sat in the back of the men's clubs on Saturday nights while I danced to make sure I didn't hold out any cash. They would keep track of all lap dances and calculate the tips I earned. Or was I just being paranoid? I knew he needed his walk-around time, but I never found out if he was actually cheating on me.

It was then that my life sort of lost its thrill. It was just a cold business arrangement. I decided it was time to do something really off the hook!

I had $1,058 and a thirty-day pass, so I took a bus out of town. I just packed a bag and my backpack and did a code seven. I left a note telling Beckley that I needed some time to myself. I was smart enough to give notice to the gentlemen's clubs where I danced; there was no need to burn my bridges.

Mom was not happy with my leaving and kept telling me to come back home. She worried about me being on the road. For about twenty-five days, I traveled. I went to Newport, Boston, Salem, Buffalo, Niagara Falls, Chicago, Milwaukee, St. Paul, and Indianapolis, and then I slowly worked my way back to New York with a fresh perspective. During my travels, I met some nice people. I found I loved traveling.

I enjoyed seeing new sites and cities and meeting new people who were in transit. Unfortunately, I got homesick and lovesick. I had a few intimate moments with guys I met on the bus, but they only made me want Beckley more than ever. More than that, I wanted desperately to get back to the way things had been. I was ready to give him a baby if he wanted. I just wanted him back. I needed him. I was going to make sure that Beckley and I got back to the relationship we had at one time. I wanted him to love me again, and I would do just about anything to achieve the love that we had before. I was tempted to call ahead, but I decided a surprise was best. My mistake! It was all different when I arrived at the Port Authority Terminal.

It was mid-October and unseasonably chilly in New York City when I returned. The locks had been changed on our apartment door, so I grabbed a cab to Mom's place. I walked over to a café we used to frequent and found him there. He was eating French fries with ketchup and a cup of coffee with a close friend. Beckley acted totally indifferent, as if it were just another dull day. He didn't even acknowledge me or ask me how my trip was.

As we stepped out of the café, I hugged him and started crying. "You are making this hard for me." He kissed me on the lips, but there was no intention or passion. My heart sank. In the brief few weeks I was away, the loss of my income meant that he was forced to find employment. He had called in a marker to Hector and gotten a job as a forklift driver at a warehouse. The BMW was broken, and it was going to cost more than $2,500 to get it fixed.

Beckley had also found himself a new girl, Angela. She was nineteen years old and claimed she had been a working girl since age eleven. Angela was a loud, petite, double alpha female type. She was street-hardened and spoke her mind, even in mixed company. She spoke with a classic heavy Latin accent.

Vantessa on a leash

Like the weather, Beckley was cold toward me. He mostly ignored me. He let me visit the apartment sometimes. It was obvious I was demoted. If we were watching movie or a game, he sat with Angela, and they basically ignored me. The writing was on the wall, and I was heartbroken. I was glad that I moved back in with my mom. She was glad to have me back.

I humbly accepted my lowered status, feeling it was my fault for leaving him on short notice. I thought he would somehow understand and take me back if I played it straight with him. Maybe it would be better than before.

I was wrong, lovesick, and didn't eat. I went back to dancing. I hoped his ill feelings toward me would be temporary. Angela was outwardly hostile to me. She considered me a threat. She openly said she would pay him the equivalent of $3,500 to buy me so she could turn me and pimp me out properly. I ignored her. Beckley wouldn't allow that, would he?

Despite my efforts to be cordial to Beckley's current friend Angela, she continued acting like a bitch. She had his total support, so I accepted her abusive attitude—but only to point. I was eight inches taller and outweighed her by forty pounds. I got ready for a fight.

Walking on eggshells, I sensed Beckley kept me hanging on by a thread. I was lonely for him on the road and wanted to get back, to recapture the warmth and sense of belonging. I wanted that hair-pulling, bum-smacking, harpooned-from-behind kind of love. I learned to really like that kind of treatment. I had grown used to it. I needed him so badly. He rejected me by not embracing me. At other times, Beckley acted as if he just needed time to accept me back. He was neutral. It was killing me. I was beginning to doubt myself.

It was cruel of him to hold back. He wouldn't say yes, and he wouldn't say no. It was like that old Supremes song: "Set me free, why don't you, babe."

As far as I was concerned, Beckley was the only game in town, and I needed him. I should have known better, but I crawled back to him, tail between my legs, only to find indifference. I had only $26.05 left.

To Beckley, I was merely an ATM machine. He was no longer interested in keeping me. Only the money mattered to him. I immediately went back to dancing full-time, as it was something I could easily fall back on. Believe it or not, exotic dancing is a skill, and I was able to find employment as a dancer, hostess, or waitress nearly every place I ventured.

Meanwhile, life became unbearable. The silence between us was deafening. I was treated more like an acquaintance than a friend. Still, I went to work four or five nights each week.

I kept nearly all of my earnings away from Beckley. I hid some mad money, but it was never enough. I realized this situation was going to deteriorate even more. I was yesterday's news. I was heartbroken but reluctantly accepted it. We were through; it was time to move on.

Teaching Vantessa a new routine

I hoped he would warm up to me again if I kept feeding him money. With Angela always hovering nearby, it was nearly impossible to spend any real quality time with Beckley. I had no idea what kind of relationship he and Angela had going. I didn't care. I gave him some pocket money when I saw him from time to time. During the day, we always seemed to bump into each other at the weirdest times and places. It was maddening and fueled false hopes.

I made sure to squirrel away a few dollars so I could more comfortably leave, and I had some help. There were some gentlemen at the clubs who sympathized with me. I danced for these guys, treated them kindly, and they made small donations to help me escape from my situation in New York. They called it my college fund. I received numerous offers to be a kept woman or companion in Canada, the Middle East, Mexico, or another state. Each day was another reminder that I had failed. I wanted Beckley back, not a strange new relationship. No rebounds for me. Goodbye, all!

I didn't have much, but I left New York anyway in late January. It wasn't too difficult, really. I left for work as usual, but instead of going to work, I went to the Port Authority, hopped on an express bus, and headed for a new life in sunny California. I cannot remember if it took two or three nights, but it was warm and pleasant when the bus pulled in for a rest stop in Sacramento. My first impression of California was that it was a new world with palm trees and mild January weather.

I had met some free spirits along the way. Some were my age; some had children already or were traveling to see their military man in other parts of the country. I actually helped change a diaper on a moving bus. Meeting new people and riding to new places helped to bolster my spirits. I was not alone. Young people everywhere were living their lives, struggling to make a better place for themselves, or visiting friends and relatives.

A cheerful cadre of college kids who were headed to a ski weekend near Lake Tahoe (Squaw Valley?) invited me to join them. I am not a skier, but it did sound like great fun. I found a gift shop with an antique public telephone on H Street. I called my mom from there just to let her know I was all right. She of course told me to turn around and come right home. After a tearful phone call, I said goodbye and continued to travel further west.

The older man sitting next to me on the bus flirted with me and gave me his number. The man called himself Peg Leg, as he was missing one, but he had a million stories to tell. Each one of his recollections was more fascinating and amusing then the last. He had once put cayenne pepper into a large bag of weed his kids had purchased. When they took a hit from the pipe, it was hilarious! All I really knew was that he was married, had two college-age children, and liked to put vodka in his coffee. He kept me in stitches for many miles.

Upon arrival in Oakland on Sunday morning, I very sensibly got a cup of coffee and a hamburger platter at the cafe inside the bus station. It felt like a place inhabited by extraterrestrials. I had no plan.

# New Start: Confession #6

Mr. Curtis, Mr. Robert, and Mr. Tyrone Jackson all tried to sign on as my new pimp, but they finally realized I was a no-go. Mr. Curtis was smooth and flattered me with sappy metaphors about how beautiful I was. Mr. Robert was more businesslike. He asked if I needed a job and place to stay. Mr. Tyrone Jackson explained that he was from DC and recently moved to the Golden State to stake his claim, and would I mind going along to help him?

They were mostly looking for lone white runaway girls who might need a friend in a new town. I sipped my coffee, but I was too worn out to eat the cheeseburger platter I ordered. I had no idea where I was going to stay. I was just living for the day and totally exhausted.

A nineteen-year-old white guy with a high-end SLR camera around his neck introduced himself as Mark and told me he had been watching me handle myself with those three desperados, as he called them. He kindly asked if he could have my hamburger platter if I wasn't going to eat it. I shrugged and pushed it toward him. I silently waited for his imminent sales pitch, but it never came. He smothered the cheeseburger with ketchup (yuck!) and made casual conversation. He told me he had just gotten back from Verdi, Nevada and claimed he had been pearl diving in a casino in Reno, Nevada. He was staying in San Francisco with friends near Fisherman's Wharf, and … blah, blah, blah.

I asked him what he meant by pearl diving in Reno. He said that he gambled all his money away and then had to wash dishes to earn some gas money so he could make his return trip. I don't know if any of it was true, because I recalled that there was still quite a bit of snow in the mountains near the California-Nevada border. The boy did not stop talking. He asked me my age. I asked, "How old do you think I am?" He surprised me by saying twenty-seven, even though I was only nineteen. I innocently asked him how he knew. I think he felt like he had earned some brownie points for an accurate guess of my age.

Mark had light brown hair, a bubbling personality, and an upbeat attitude. He brought me out of my funk. He offered me a hot bath and a place to crash with his friend in the city. I knew nothing about San Francisco, but my instincts told me it might be all right. I still had my straight razor in my shoe.

The meal didn't go to waste, and Mark turned out to be the perfect contact for a girl who basically ran away from her home, as it turned out. He was a free spirit from a single-parent home like me. We had something in common right away. He might have been an angel sent by God. After inhaling my burger platter, he put my lone suitcase in a locker and handed me the key, and I climbed on the back of his motorcycle. It was my first ride on a Harley.

The trip across the Bay Bridge was a cold, windy, scary affair. I could tell he was holding on tight, and I held onto him. Each time the bike hit the steel bridge joints, it kind of jerked the handle bars a tiny bit. The crosswind was incredible. We rode acros that bridge tilted slightly to the port side. Riding bitch on a Harley FXDL—that's how I would arrive in San Francisco. Yahoo! Once in San Francisco, I noticed it was sunny and foggy, cool and tranquil. Sun rays cut through the fog like a beacon. I felt renewed and reborn. The City by the Bay welcomed me to a new life.

Mark was gracious. He introduced me to his friends in the Richmond District (which has since become New Chinatown) on 7ᵗʰ Avenue, just off Clement Street. I managed a hot bath and a bowl of lentil soup with parmesan cheese and sourdough bread. It was heavenly and therapeutic. Chamomile tea mixed with peppermint became my favorite. For the first time in a while, I felt human again.

Mark then escorted me to a place near Union Street where I could crash for a few days. He introduced me to Henri (pronounced "on-ree"). A dark-skinned French Canadian, Henri was the man who owned the Victorian-style home currently under renovation. Henri had painted a fantastic mural on his living room wall right next to his babies which, of course, were his botanically cultivated and manicured pot plants. He was playing "China Girl" by David Bowie on his sound system. The myriad painted fantasy characters were depictions of his friends. It was an excellent fantasy mural and looked pretty cool. He inspired me. I couldn't help but ask to show him some of my own art from my sketchbook. We had good chemistry and hit it off pretty well.

Henri gave me the key to a vacant upstairs apartment under the condition that I strip some old paint off the wood molding to earn my keep. He had purchased the hundred-year-old Victorian on the cheap and was giving it a good renovation; I set up my place on the carpet, next to the space heater. I stayed there for about a week and stripped a lot of paint before pressing onward.

It wasn't hard getting a dancing job. The nightlife on the Broadway strip and in the Tenderloin district in San Francisco is fairly robust. Turnover of personnel seemed pretty high, which helped maintain abundant job openings. I found work within two days. I felt like a success already.

I found it to be a haven for transgender folk. I was used to gay people in New York City, but in San Francisco, it is all out in the open. Imagine two girls getting on the bus. One is dressed in a yellow consignment store dress and the other in a matching orange dress. Both of them look rough and sport beards. They engage in an insult contest, and the riders on the bus (myself included) feel like we are watching a tennis match. Before we get to Market Street from the Haight, even the bus driver is laughing briskly.

Remind me never to get into an argument with those guys—holy cow. Imagine sitting at a bar and not really being sure if you were chatting with a guy or a girl. And it didn't matter. These were people with feelings, dreams, and intellect. I had intimate conversations with people who came from a normal Midwestern upbringing and then came to San Francisco to live their lives as completely different people. The butterfly effect changed my point of view in many ways. It is like learning about another truth that you didn't think of before but always agreed with in your heart.

The experiences made me think differently about the topic. I admit I curiously dipped into the bisexual lifestyle just for the expereince, but that is a story for another time. I was invited to an invite-only party at a nightclub, and once inside, the organizers bolted the door. I went as Henri's guest.

I was introduced to go-go boys that evening. Yes! Imagine Greek gods. These guys were ripped and perfectly toned. As the music blared, these guys would shake tambourines *(chicka-chicka-chicka-chicka!)* and then take a snort from a tiny glass or silver flask on a necklace. They took a whiff and then continued again, shaking their stuff in their loincloths and banging their tambourines. I made eye contact with one of them, and he smiled back and shook his stuff for me suggestively. I had never seen go-go boys before.

I was introduced to Gary the go-go boy and Grand Marnier that night. It poured for free all night long. I was surprised to discover that I was the only girl in the entire place. Gary, the go-go boy I had flirted with, danced with me in his loin cloth, right on the dance floor. It was hilarious. He was simply gorgeous, but I could tell that his better days were all behind him. He explained the whippets he was sniffing due to his boredom with his job, and that kind of killed whatever hopes of getting laid that night I had harbored.

Attached to the cat bell

The entire club was packed to the gills. Liquor kept flowing, and Gary was my buddy for the night. At one point, I had an urge, and I was just loose and tipsy enough to throw caution to the wind. I asked if I could go down on him, right there on the dance floor. He lifted his loin cloth, and I sank to my knees and gave that sweaty Greek god a sweet sucking. The rest of the intoxicated dancers on the stage kept on dancing while I went downtown. I never saw him after that night, although he promised to see me dance at the Cabaret.

I found San Francisco to be an open city. There is so much culture there. I was trying new things, like yoga, aikido, cooking for myself, and fencing—and all within my first month. After my first couple of interviews, I had secured two dancing jobs. That was a good thing, because I put all of my extra money on a cash deposit for a small but refurbished apartment on Haight Street. It was a one-room efficiency apartment with a small kitchen, a closet, and a bathroom. It was $165 per month over my budget, but it had a brand-new hardwood floor. It overlooked a small nightclub and was only one block from Golden Gate Park. I settled into the famed Haight Ashbury.

Mark came to see me periodically. He turned out to be one hell of a nice guy and a good friend. He was a serious liberal and a political science major; he wrote poetry and loved all music from Earth, Wind & Fire. I sensed that he carried a torch for me, although he was either too afraid to commit or too timid to come forward with his feelings. We settled for late-night motorcycle rides along the coast followed by coffee and carrot cake. If he had just slapped or spanked me one time, I would have gushed in my pants for him. He was plainly too nice of a guy, and that's what killed the romantic component between us. I go for bad boys! I always have.

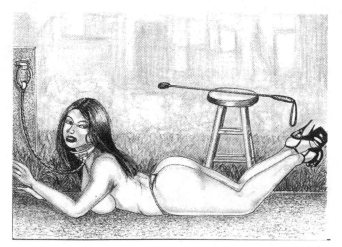

Anticipation of the caning was worse than the caning itself.

Mark and I connected once in a blue moon. He brought a board game, Chinese food, and/or a new music album over with every visit. He would park his motorcycle under my window, and I would make ginseng tea or coffee, or on cold nights, heat some red wine and put sliced fruit in it. Silly boy! He would always wait until after I got out of the shower to ask if I wanted to make love. Argh!

That boy knew how to give a full-body massage, though. He had the touch. His fingers could put me to sleep with a nice head massage or provoke me to all-out sexual fervor. We slept together on two occasions, but he never really came on to me. The sex was wonderful, and it was the first time I actually enjoyed anal intercourse.

We smoked, drank tea, and talked for hours until he lit incense and a plum candle and placed a sleeping bag on the floor. I would massage him, and he would return the favor. He was quite particular about body creams. He preferred one titled Sun, and I liked Bambi on my skin. At the time, I didn't know why we didn't take our relationship further. Perhaps we both subconsciously knew it wouldn't work. That was the extent of our continued intimacy. It was fine.

San Francisco is a unique city. In a way, it is perfectly compact. You can be anywhere in the city in about fifteen to twenty minutes. The New York of the West Coast is San Francisco, not Los Angeles. It was there that I was reborn. It is always cool, breezy, and foggy outside, and the air in Golden Gate Park smells of eucalyptus, intoxicatingly fresh. I wish I could bottle and sell the air from Golden Gate Park. It was an enjoyable six months living one block from the panhandle.

Everybody in San Francisco is from somewhere else, it seems. I met quite a few folks from New York who were mostly from Long Island. I confided in only a few people. In the back of my mind, I was worried that somehow, my past would catch up with me or that Beckley would find me again. He was crossed off my dance card. Beckley and I would see each other again, many years later. I legally had my last name changed to Tillotson. Then I found out it was all on public record, anyway—double argh!

After a few short weeks, I got a driver's license. This was a milestone achievement for me. I did it all on my own. I saved up and bought a small ten-year-old Toyota for $2000. The compact car was not a thing of beauty, but it was reliable, and it was mine! It had a five-speed transmission, and it was great fun running through the gears up and down San Francisco's forty-six hills. Freedom!

I began to explore outside the city. I visited Sausalito, San Rafael, San Mateo, Redwood City, Big Sur, Monterey, Carmel, La Honda, and even further south. In six months, I would move again. Every six months, I moved. It just happened; I did not plan it that way.

In short order, I was making a living on my own in sunny, foggy California, and it was a good life. I lived in my own place, paid my own bills, and met and said goodbye to many good people. I survived for weeks on loaded avocado sandwiches (with Monterrey Jack and alfalfa sprouts) on sourdough bread with a side of raspberry yogurt or lentil soup. I was turning into a full-blown neo-native Californian. I let my hair grow long and natural, practiced Thai cooking and photography, and learned how to throw a Frisbee.

At first, I couldn't throw a Frisbee without having to climb in the bushes to fetch it out after every throw. Luckily, there was an observant and quite irritated eleven-year-old boy who offered his disc-throwing teachings. He gave me some basic tips, and soon I was able to play catch and throw. That young man taught me multiple techniques and helped me practice. His parents introduced me to Frisbee (disc) golf. I won the first disc golf game I ever played. There was no stopping me after that.

That's what he was thinking!

I found that I was actually pretty fair at throwing golf discs, even though I do not throw them the conventional way. My throwing technique has been dubbed "the overhand flip." I liked throwing golf discs because it is free. It's also fun to hit your target, and they glide through the air so beautifully. The sport itself is not too rugged unless you have to climb into the brush or water to retrieve an errant disc. It should be noted that most disc golfers sleep-in, leaving the course open to you and the other indigenous life forms that live there. Since then, I have become quite an avid disc golfer. I have achieved a hole-in-one (called an ace) and have played on thirty-one different courses in five different states. Not bad for a girl, huh?

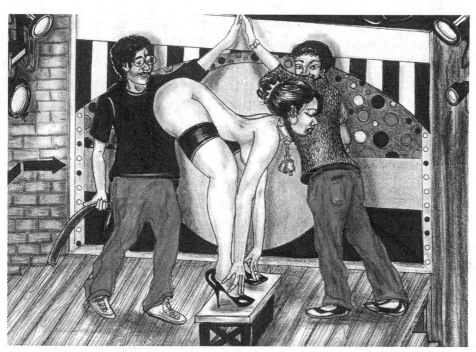

The hit of the show

After having some lucky experiences, I felt pretty successful. I was in good standing with the adult entertainment network again, but in the Bay Area this time. I had a pretty good idea of where the money and nicer clubs were. I studied the layout and located the men's clubs sprinkled liberally throughout the bay. Working on the Broadway strip was like a never-ending party, and the hustle was always on.

When not stripping, I tried my hand at graphic design and illustration, but the jobs were far apart, and it was always something that anyone with an old Wacom tablet or graphics program could whip up in a minute. Through word of mouth, I acquired some underground art jobs. I designed an album cover for a local band, a mural on a wall in Oakland, and a few illustrations for local Bay Area periodicals. I visited Last Gasp Commix frequently to get inspiration and quiet comic book reading time. I did receive one professional art job drawing majestic redwood trees. The product I created was then published in a highly renowned San Francisco-based internationally distributed environmental magazine. I temped, helped out at the corner store, and started dating again. I stayed busy.

I dated a married man for while (who claimed he was separated from his ex). I met him at the club where I worked. He took me to a 49ers game. There is something special about being in the VIP section and seeing the action from there. The affair was short-lived, unfortunately. There were also a few outings to the fashionable nightclubs and fine restaurants. I even stayed a night at the famed St. Francis Hotel with him. Divorce in California is usually super-expensive for the man. I do not judge people. Life was good. I was merely performing a service—at least, that was what I kept telling myself. Is monogamy an unnatural act? From my experience, men want their home and security yet live like they are single and free. I quit the dating scene for a while and took GED classes.

While riding on the BART train one day, I got a hot tip to show up and try out for the cheerleading squad for the Oakland Raiders football team. Needless to say, I was there, standing in line, before the sun came up. The day of tryouts was a long and painstaking one. I was amazed how many girls and even mature ladies were applying. Making the second cut was encouraging to me, and I thought for sure my ship had at last come in. It was not meant to be, however. On the third cut, I didn't quite perform on all eight cylinders and was dismissed.

I was just out of sync. The coordinators did offer me a chance to come back and try again the following year, and that is when I started crying. My real problem is that I always do things my way, not necessarily the way that they are supposed to be accomplished. That includes dancing—and everything about me, really. I seem to always zig when everyone else zags. When everything is in balance, I seem to just want to jangle the scale again. That is just me.

Growing restless, I decided to explore further south. Southern California is a totally different country in many respects. I was always pretty careful, but one day, I went to an actual redwood forest preserve with an amorous young couple, Bill and Rose. Rose was a technical consultant, and Bill was a student. They were both Elvis Costello fanatics, and I found myself singing along to the song "Red Shoes." These two individuals were polar opposites, a Libra and an Aries—so much so that they were absolutely perfect for each other. They complimented each other to a tee. Rose was the matriarchal type, and Bill was the adventurous fool.

On a weekend road trip to San Mateo, we got high and drove into the redwood forest. We drove to a secluded location deep among those giants. We had a threesome on a picnic table under the splendor of those magnificent Sequoia trees. The air in that forest was pure and fragrant, like a dream world. It was the closest I have ever been to heaven on earth. Our small orgy was initiated by the very horny Rose. She removed her clothes, unzipped Bill, and opened my blouse. It was spontaneous and very different from anything I had experienced before.

Purring.

Later that evening, at their Diamond Heights apartment, we made an amateur porn movie. It was all accomplished in candlelight and turned out okay. It was all right;

we were in the straight missionary position, but that was not what I had expected to do with my weekend.

As fate would have it, I also ended up going to a nude beach with a fellow colleague, Rachel, who is a red-haired beauty with fair skin. I wasn't sure how long she would last out there under that sun. It was Memorial Day, and we brought margaritas with us in a cooler.

We left the city in her '67 Dodge Dart early to beat traffic along the coastal highway. I had never been to one before but loved it immediately. In California, in many places, you have to climb down into the beach, not just walk up to it. It was incredibly scenic. Huge cliffs and rocks that had broken from the mainland were pounded by the splashing surf. Like in the movies, the waves crashed on the rocks. I could see crustaceans in the tide pools after we made the trek down into the rocky, sandy basin below. The warm California sun felt wonderful. It wasn't too hot, even though the sun was bright. A fine mist rolled in over the beach as we placed our blankets down and soaked up some rays.

It was just my friend and I for a while as the hazy mist from the Pacific Ocean floated in, making the sun feel less brutal. A short time later, we discovered a guy nearby soaking up the sun. He was olive-skinned with wavy blonde hair (a golden Adonis type) who rushed up to me on his way out and handed me a cocktail napkin with a hastily-scratched phone number. He said that if I ever wanted to be a model to call him. And with that, he added, "It would be to your advantage to contact me." Yeah, right! Nice try, though.

This was the same guy who for two hours was posed on the beach in such a manner that all his stuff pointed right at us. He was trying to make it look like it was just coincidental, but the self-satisfied smirk on his face betrayed him. Rachel commented on the obvious taunting exposure. We laughed and joked that he was going to get it sunburned. It was obvious he knew that we knew he was doing this all on purpose. I tried not look too often, and every time I did, he had that same grin on his face. He knew I was peeping at his peepee. Then he gave me his phone number as he scampered up the wooden stairway on the canyon wall.

San Francisco is a cosmic place. It is not of this earth. It is basically a small town. It is nearly a perfect seven-by-seven-mile square. I am not certain, but I believe that is where the term 49er comes from—either that, or the gold rush of 1849. During the day, it has maybe 1.6 million people there. Only 870,000 culturally diverse residents actually live there.

What were the odds? Ironically, I saw this same young man, fully clothed, driving a faded yellow Ford Econoline van that very next day. It was right after lunch time at the corner of Montgomery and Market Streets. I was on my way back toward the Embarcadero from Macy's, and there he was. That same boy! We both looked at each other in disbelief.

He had just dropped someone off. She looked like she could have been his potential squeeze. She was wearing an immaculately tailored black pinstriped business suit and holding a leather organizer under her arm. She was Asian and very attractive, and every hair on her head was perfectly in place. She looked around quizzically, as she detected that something was up, and I quickly looked away and kept walking. It was like the twilight zone. She looked around like, "What's going on here?" We were rock and roll in a fraction of a second. That strange boy, the golden Adonis with the sunburned penis, caught up with me moments later in his van and motioned with a shake of his head for me to climb in the van.

I don't know what made me do it; maybe it was curiosity. I quickly jumped in the van, just like that. I got into a stranger's van with my packages. I wanted to know more about this handsome interloper. We made introductions, and he told me his name was Ken. He asked me if I would have coffee with him. I told him he would have to take me to a predetermined bus stop afterward, and he drove me to a coffee house off Mission Street.

I thought this was an okay way to break the ice, since we had never seen each other before yesterday. Wow! And here he was, in close proximity, twice in two days. What was up with that? He came right out and asked, "What is it with you?"

"I could ask the same question, right?" I retorted. I almost came out and asked him about his sunburned tally whacker. I held back but kept it in my back pocket in case I needed it for conversation.

The coffee house smelled wonderful, and the coffee was rich. The entire cafe featured chessboards at the tables. We played a casual game of chess while we sipped our espressos. When we ran out of things to say, we just concentrated on the game and the next chess move. Perfect. Nice move, Ken.

Later that afternoon, we found ourselves sipping sweet French merlot and doing it doggy-style in a carpeted third-floor apartment on Beulah Street. Ken was a very good-looking man. He was not the kind of guy I would be interested in, because he looked to be really into himself. No one would ever believe we only met briefly yesterday. I am not sure how we ended up doing the wild thing on his floor in front of the massive bay windows, but it started with one kiss. Then came some light petting and then more kissing. My blouse and bra somehow came off, and the next thing I knew, I was being impaled in front of those bay windows. He pulled my hair and spanked me as he rammed the old avenger home repeatedly.

I looked up at Sutro Tower as I came. I was wondering how tall it was, because right then and there, I was one hundred miles above it! Wow! It was so much fun that I had to ask for seconds by kissing him back to erect status. He laid with his head and shoulders on a large colorful pillow while I rode him like a cowgirl trying to tame a bucking bronco. I was just about to soar above Sutro Tower again when Miss Immaculate with the black pinstriped suit walked in on us!

I looked up and stopped. Ken looked up and said, "Hey! Glad you are home! This is Vantessa! Vantessa, this is Thai." I nodded awkwardly, still impaled on Ken's turgid shaft.

She unbuttoned her suit jacket and said, "Jesus, Ken, can't you do it in your room? For God's sake!" Then she disgustedly left us, presumably to go to her room. What a pill.

We resumed our scandalous copulation in front of the bay windows, basking in the afternoon sunshine, just savoring the ride right next to a large planter of colorful flowers. One month later, I replaced his upwardly mobile roomie. She reportedly moved to Mill Valley. I never asked if they were lovers. He didn't tell.

Now here was a guy I only met briefly, didn't care for, and then—wham! The very next day, he was banging me from behind in his living room. And one month later, I moved in with the Ken. Physically, he was everything I could ever want. He had olive brown skin like an Italian; yet even the fine hairs on his knuckles were blonde. He was in excellent shape and looked like he could take care of himself. I liked that.

After strawberry pancakes and chamomile tea on Saturday mornings, we rode bicycles into the Presidio with a spectacular view of the Golden Gate. Then we rode onward to Fisherman's Wharf. We checked out the wares of the street artists, observed the tourists on Beach Street, and then enjoyed a traditional Irish coffee at the Buena Vista Café. From there, we biked past the marina and over the Golden Gate Bridge itself.

Once on the other side of the bay, we stopped to take a few scenic pictures of the fog slowly rolling over the hills like a white cotton blanket. It was there that we observed a powder blue Rolls Royce convertible with a dashing young man and a gorgeous woman sitting on the hood. Before them on the hood was a backgammon board. We watched as they played for a minute. The rather attractive woman on the hood of that magnificent mountain of a car briefly explained how to play it and also how addictive it can be. Backgammon is the world's cruelest game. If you play, you know why.

Further on down toward Sausalito, we stopped to enjoy a glass of wine and then coasted down to the Sausalito strip for some rocky road on a sugar cone. We placed our bikes in the rack of the ferry boat around sunset and set sail for a return trip to San Francisco once again. Ken ordered us drinks as twilight descended upon us. The city skyline lit up in the morning of the gods. We were just a stone's throw from Alcatraz Island. It was a romantic cruise back to the city.

On Sundays, we rode bicycles in the rain to a place tucked away in the hills of Noe Valley. With our combined incomes and a roommate, we could afford to live in a fairly nice restored Victorian flat. I moved with him. We now lived in Noe Valley, which is one of the rare places where it is partially sunny most all of the time. The fog has a hard time getting into the cleverly situated Noe Valley area near Mission Delores Park. Noe Valley has a near perfect Mediterranean climate with warm summer days and cool, wet winters.

My new man Ken enjoyed snapping pictures of me as a hobby. I never knew when he would ambush me with that damn camera of his. I didn't mind, really, until he began mounting nude photos of me on the wall. He took lots of pictures of me, and I soon became his favorite photographic study. He taught me about the beauty of high-contrast black-and-white imaging, lighting, depth of field, and other technical features. Ken was not a photographer but a photographic artist. The first time he photographed me, I was unsuspectingly coming out of the shower.

Ken knew what I did for a living, but he never complained. Many times, he drove me in to work and gave me luscious kisses in the parking lot. I think he did it to show everyone that I was his girl. I didn't mind. He often picked me up after my shift too. I felt safe, and it saved wear and tear on my car and fuel expenses. It was nice having a normal relationship with a man. He didn't seem to mind that I was a dancer. For the first time in my life, I felt settled. It was real. Unfortunately, restlessness eventually overcame both of us, and six months later, we parted ways, agreeing it was best.

Leaving the Bay Area in my dust, I moved south after cashing in my chips. I apologized profusely to my employers (who were unexpectedly kind and understanding). For the next year or so, I ended up bouncing around Los Angeles, going from one Mr. Wrong to the next. A bunch of mama's boys, trying to find themselves—excuse me?

I met a girl named Carrie at an audition. We were both hired as dancers at a hip club in Malibu. I liked the area—close to the water with nice hills nearby. This is the California I think of when I hear a Beach Boys song. I met up with this skinny nineteen-year-old girl from Panama, who was born on the very same day I was, while awaiting an interview with the manager of the Celestials Men's Club. She had a captivating Libra charm about her and smiled with a full mouth of crisp white teeth. She had perky little tits (which have since been enhanced), mocha skin like mine, and one of the most perfectly rounded asses I have ever seen.

We became friends instantly. She was always in a good mood. We applied for jobs together and got hired at the same club. We watched each other's backs. For a while, we were sisters. We danced at the Celestials Club, which at that time was considered an upscale, white-collar gentleman's club. It was party time! We were quite fortunate to be able to find a loft apartment in Malibu, about six blocks from the beach. I am certain the landlord was smitten by Carrie's smile, which sealed the deal.

I do not know if she is still making films, but Carrie M. was one of the most sought-after and highly-paid porn actresses ever. She could and would do anything and cheerfully convince you she loved it. She always went the extra mile for people in her life. She was a gem of a lady. She had an angel's smile, and being a gorgeous Libra, she had dimples to die for. She possessed a gift for making you feel important, even when just saying hello. Her smile would disarm anyone in an instant.

Carrie recently had a complete makeover that only amplified her beauty. I was mildly jealous for a while that she was living my dream. But she deserves her fame and fortune. She would later come to my rescue and do a huge favor for me. That is a story for another time. She enriched me and made me wonder how much love a person can have in their heart. That is just who she was to me. God sends us nothing but angels.

We both applied and were called out to modeling jobs, and at the ripe old age of twenty-two, we both made really good money. That was a summer that completely gave itself over to us. We were hot, in our prime, and working at a really nice men's club in a great location. It was perfect. Was there more to be achieved?

Together, we rode a wave of good fortune. Work was fun and lucrative. We knew in our hearts it would only get better and last forever. She became my best friend. We easily pulled in thousands on some nights. We both got pulled into the spoils and did not get much sleep, smoked too much, tooting and hanging out under the influence instead of planning and plotting our next career moves. Success can test you just as harshly as poverty.

With my newfound popularity and prosperity, I naturally tried to expand my network portfolio even more. I had bought the California dream! I took acting lessons and kept myself groomed and manicured. Through the clientele at the club, I was introduced to the Newport Beach swingers scene. It seemed perfect. Connecting to a higher level on the food chain made me think increased wealth could be at hand. After short time, I was once again bored. The water was shallow.

Partying and working the clubs was like living a Robert Earle Keene song: *"The road goes on forever, and the party never ends."* I observed other girls getting caught up in it. They were hustling, going to hotels with clients they met at the club, earning some fast cash and then spending it on drugs. Then they repeated the vicious cycle again the following weekend. They were girls who lived to party. I was lucky in that I never became ensnared in that scene. I managed to avoid any real setbacks not of my own making.

At age twenty-two, I left Malibu and moved to Redondo Beach for a while. I had said goodbye to my sister from another mother, Carrie, but we pledged we would see each other periodically.

I moved in with a blonde surfer girl, Michele, originally from Shoreham, Long Island. She came from a fairly well-to-do family, had a great sense of humor, and liked to surf and party every day. She was shorter than me but a tad stockier and practically lived on the beach.

I had retired from dancing and decided to live off my savings while considering a career in graphic design. I bought a drawing table, illustration board, and desktop computer with information superhighway capability, some basic CAD software, and a scanner and printer. I created a business calling card of my own design and set about to make my fortune as a graphic artist for hire.

Sometimes business was slow. Art and modeling jobs were sporadic at best. I eventually tired of not having a job to go to every day. I put on my thong and heels again and got back into a men's club. It was a double-edged sword. I knew how to get hired as a dancer; yet I didn't wish to do it full time. Unfortunately, I have a terrible character flaw. I can't say no. Being needed and desired means a lot to me as a person. Soon I was dancing full time again.

My roomie, Michele, had a brilliant idea. She was going to rent a large boat, have a band play on it, and take paying customers on a two- or three-hour cruise. It would be a cruise along the coast with music, finger foods, and champagne for everyone. She needed to sell about sixty tickets at $120 per ticket to make a profit on the excursion costs. It was her dream to promote the cruise. I enjoy a good boat ride myself, especially at night when the moon is out. It all sounded good to me, and I offered to do the advertising for it. A friend of mine found an available top-forty contemporary band, and we signed them. I set out to design a flyer, a poster, and a newspaper advertisement and get it on the market.

I took great care to design an art deco motif of a beautiful cruise ship under the moon in placid waters with tropical islands in the foreground and background. I paid for the camera-ready prints and inter-negatives to publish and launch our media blitz.

As I was doing this, Michele was meeting up with some new friends. These so-called friends were in the cocaine business. She was partaking and partying with them. One evening, she came home and explained that she had a new band set up for the cruise. They were a band of her cocaine friends, of course. I had met them once and didn't particularly care for them. They seemed to talk a good story, but my spider sense told me they were amateur at best. They also carried guns, which made me nervous.

All of the art I had completed was thrown in the trash because she didn't inform me of this abrupt change. With a calm exterior, I took it in stride and changed the name of the band, silently cursing under my breath. Tickets were being sold, and money was coming in. The $1500 deposit to reserve the boat had already been made. Everything appeared to be on track.

Unknown to me, Michele was spending the money that was coming in on cocaine and alcohol. When I found out, I washed my hands of it. I had accomplished my end of the bargain. I published the artwork and marketing, as promised. I invested quite a bit of my own time and money into this project. I was out!

The very next night, I was at home and finishing up a yearlong project—my first oil painting. I was in a celebratory mood as I put the final strokes on the painting. I opened a bottle of wine and admired my art piece. Just then, Michele came in, and she was in a mood to fight. She ranted, and I could tell she had been drinking. She attacked me. I was larger, stronger, and a better fighter. I bested her and pushed her out the door of our apartment. A few moments later, I heard a crash!

She actually crashed through a glass window, flying into my room a short time later, breaking the window above my bed. She was cut from the glass, and she pulled a buck knife out and threatened me with it. I ran to the kitchen and pulled a bigger knife out, and we stood there, facing each other. After a minute of facing each other off, she threw the knife into the floor near my feet. I pulled it out of the floor, opened the back door, and threw it out into the night. Our physical catfight resumed. I broke a bone in my right hand from pummeling her face. I made her leave again after she tapped out.

The apartment was trashed. My stereo system was broken. A pitcher of orange juice was upside down on the floor; it was nearly full and didn't appear to have spilled a drop. I rummaged through her personal telephone book and called her parents on Long Island. At the same time, her ex-boyfriend walked into the house, saying, "Michele said you cut her with a knife, and she is bleeding." Two of the biggest police officers I have ever seen were right behind him. I thought to myself, I am going to jail.

The officers asked me what had transpired, and I explained it. They asked me what I wanted to do. I said, "Make her stay here and sleep it off." I ended up going home with her ex-boyfriend, who let me sleep on his couch. I called a mover the next morning and moved out.

In a way, the fight was a good thing. I had to reflect on my life. I was twenty-two years old and at the crossroads. I needed to either get my shit together or continue the path I was on. Luckily, I had the smarts to choose wisely. I went to temping again, volunteered at fashion shows, continued networking, and completed evening GED classes. I worked hard, and in three months, I received my diploma. I was back dancing again, but only to maintain that expensive new flat I had leased. I attempted modeling when I could get it. I was offered a chance to do hardcore porn but chickened out at the last second. I didn't care for the people involved. A good friend of mine advised me to avoid the porn circuit, and luckily, I had the smarts to heed her advice.

Modeling was the most fun, though. I loved being in front of a mirror or a camera. There is a connection between the model, the camera, the image, and the photographer that is hard to describe. It is like being someone else for a while. You can both lose and find yourself simultaneously while the camera shutter clicks and the flash unit recharges with a beep. It made me feel like I had hit the big-time, even if only in a minor way.

A familiar dance

# *Awakening the Beast Within: Confession #7*

I pledged to myself that I would never go back to New York. California, with all of its natural disasters, smog, and sky-high taxes and cost of living, was still way better for me. I considered myself a Californian all the way through.

One morning, I was just about to leave my apartment for the day when I received a call from an agency that was looking for a bondage model, and I took it. I drove to an industrial area near a large Budweiser factory in Van Nuys and knocked on the door.

As I waited for an answer, I was startled out of my wits by a sudden roar. A man mounted on a cherry red antique triumph motorcycle with loud pipes came from behind me.

I told the rider, a rough-looking graying man in his fifties, that he had scared me. He tossed his cigarette, stomped on it with his dirty jack boot, exhaled a lung full of smoke, and then calmly replied that the bike sometimes scares him as well. He was a rough-looking guy with stained teeth, a deep, raspy voice, and a chain-smoking habit.

As it turned out, he was the photographer I was to meet with. He led me inside and turned on the lights in his museum-like studio. There were dusty file cabinets in various states of disrepair, one old office desk from the sixties, and an array of lighting umbrellas and diffusers. He showed me neatly laminated examples of his previous work and explained the shoot in detail. I was going to be strapped in, chained up, cuffed, racked, caged, and a few other things. Dungeon-like old movie props were crammed in every corner. It appeared that real S&M stuff happened in this studio. Suddenly it occurred to me that I didn't really understand what was expected of me other than to get naked.

He regarded me, lit another smoke (his third in ten minutes), and said, "Take 'em off, and get started." I surmised that this is what it is to be a professional model. I did as I was told, and in minutes, the photo session was on. He began with some soft poses and gradually worked a collar around my neck, a ball gag into my mouth, and a pair of heavy medieval handcuffs onto my wrists. Then he tied a rope bra on me; my breasts were bound tightly to a swinging trapeze bar while I stood precariously on two cement blocks. His rope work was highly precise and quite symmetrical. He made it look easy. It not only looked expertly done, but was also quite effective. It wasn't too tight and did not cut off circulation, but it would not allow me to wiggle free or loosen it. I was effectively bound under the lights. His camera snapped away.

As the session progressed, he carefully tied me onto various bondage machines and devices. His studio was full of a wide assortment of props and dungeon-like cages and structures. He must have taken about seven hundred photos in all. I found myself getting wet and stimulated by what he did to me as the camera clicked away. That camera shutter was the only thing heard, and it echoed. Before that day, I had never been tied, chained, or placed into strict bondage in front of a camera. It slowly worked on me. I drooled from the ball gag in my mouth, and he loved it. He took a series of shots of my long strands of saliva as they dangled off my chin only to snap off onto my bulging, roped tits.

The cumulative effect of being exposed and restricted while my dirty bits were being recorded made me feel a long-forgotten tingle between my legs. That motorized camera was teasing me—dare I say, taunting me? I was getting helplessly aroused. I found it more than mildly thrilling as the shoot progressed.

Halfway through the photoshoot, I was placed on the rack and then the leg spreader. There were no insertions, which I was glad for. The rubber ball gag was the only intrusive device that day. I was very wet, and I didn't know if that was a good thing or a bad thing. Whatever that unkempt, chain-smoking, smelly, nasty old goat of a photographer wanted of me, I was eager to do for him. In fact, when he was finally through untying me and wrapping up the business of our shoot, I was practically ready to get on my knees and beg for an old-fashioned shagging. I hinted that I really enjoyed being in bondage for him. I could smell my own excitement, and I wondered if he could, too. My submissive side had been reawakened. I bit my lip and gave him an impish smile.

He lit yet another cigarette and looked at me, totally amused. He then handed me my voucher. I don't smoke but felt like asking to bum one from him. I was sexually excited, and there was no denying it. I watched him in slow motion as he walked over, collected my belongings and clothes, and then with a dismissive, cavalier expression, threw them out the door by his motorcycle. He gave me a gentle shove and said, "Thanks, kid; I'll call ya!"

Out the door I went, stumbling over my feet, nearly landing on my butt. I scuffed one of my heels. I was about to pound on his door and curse at him but realized I was naked as a jaybird in broad daylight near a busy industrial section of Van Nuys, California. Yikes! There was a lot of traffic on the streets surrounding the parking lot. My car was quite a ways away.

Still adorned with the rope marks on my tits and wrists, I was an eyeful. I got to my feet, slipped my panties on, grabbed up my clothes and purse, and scampered to a sign indicating a restroom was nearby. I ran as fast as I could shuffle my feet in five-inch heels, hoping it was available. Fortunately, it was unlocked and unoccupied. Though filthy, at least it was private. I dove inside, locked the door, and quickly tried to make myself presentable once again. I could hear horns beeping from distant cars and wondered if all that honking was for me. Moments later, I carefully emerged from the confines of that filthy restroom. When I felt the coast was clear, I replaced my heels with my sneakers and ran to my car.

Beware the no panty zone!

I was very tempted to key the gas tank on his beloved Tiger 650 motorcycle or go back into his studio and give him a piece of my mind. It wasn't the bike's fault, I reasoned. I couldn't do it. Instead, I got back in my car and drove off. My first real photoshoot. Wow! Was this what it was like? I was out of breath, and my heart pounded in my chest.

It was evident I was into bondage. I would seek it out. Lurking but dormant, my submissive side was coming to the fore again. I felt alive. I practically threw myself at the feet of that derelict photographer, and he rejected me, like he was dusting off a piece of lint on his leather jacket.

It was a good thing I didn't retaliate against the photographer, however. One month later, I received a call back to his studio. This time, the older man had a younger version of himself there with him. He was either the older man's son or an understudy. They laughed and joked about how I squirmed when racked out. The older man told the younger one about how hot and wet I had gotten during the last photoshoot. It was slightly embarrassing to be spoken of like that, especially as my legs were tied wide open on a wooden pony apparatus. I shined on, smiled, and said nothing. Boys always kiss and tell, don't they?

This time, however, I was over it. I learned my lesson. It was strictly business this time—somewhat of a disappointment to those two. Upon completion of the photoshoot, I could tell they were sizing me up, so to speak. I believe they expected me to give it up to them. I quickly grabbed my clothes and strolled out the door nude before they could react. I checked the amount on the voucher, said, "Thank you," and carried my clothes out the door to the same rather nasty restroom to dress. I could feel their eyes on me as I left.

Depending on the type of shoot and the photographer's discretion, a cooldown period is routinely required just to make sure all the body parts are nourished with blood before moving on the next restrictive setup or when leaving the studio. The only really intrusive part of this particular shoot was a vibe placed on my clitoris while I was stretched out on the rack. It was pretty much for show; there was no real penetration. I didn't let on that being in these restrictive devices was again turning me on. It was considered more of a softcore photoshoot for a magazine bondage feature. It got my motor running. That was the last I saw of that studio. I never did see the photos published.

I considered myself lucky. I had heard rumors of girls having to beg and crawl under the desk of agency executives in order to be called for a photoshoot. Quid pro quo? I had been called twice, and already I felt pretty salty. It was to be the last call to that particular bondage studio.

I learned there is basically an ocean of new and beautiful women who are looking for their big break, even in the adult entertainment industry. It appeared to me that there was an overflow of eighteen-year-old girls with birth certificates in hand (on their eighteenth birthdays, no less) applying for work as dancers and models. It would be hypocritical of me to say anything negative about that; I was doing that kind of work at eighteen.

Competition today is incredibly high. You have to be willing to do anything on demand. I was later referred to another more upscale agency that had selected the men's club where I was employed for a feature in an online expose. Evidently, this promotional group sought to exhibit dancers from various men's clubs around the world. Opportunity knocked once again.

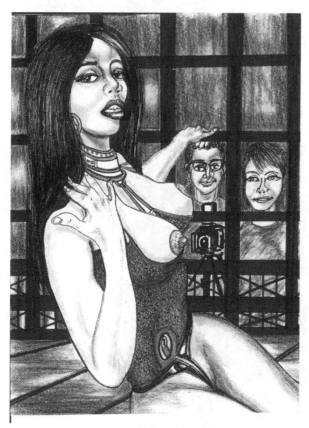

Caged and photographed

When I saw my first photo feature on screen, it was glorious—a minor victory! They named me Natalia (although I am Korean, Puerto Rican, and Creole), and lay on my stomach with my buns up, invitingly displayed in full HD resolution. The next few images contained a montage of several stock girlie-type poses—the usual stuff that most guys like. My makeup was perfect, and my skin looked golden brown and fabulous. The images posted there were very complimentary. I had arrived.

Once I found work, more opportunities presented themselves. For a while, things were once again quite good. Alas, everything good has to end. Clubs get bought and sold, management changes, the club gets shut down for a violation or moves to a new facility, and people leave. The rules and the climate of a club are in a constant flux. I had quit dancing many times and shortly after started again, but now I felt that I needed new scenery.

That's the way it went. I forwarded my resume all over town. I was called on to become an escort after qualifying for the honor (with five interviews). I attended functions and went on dates with businessmen. It wasn't all that easy, really. It was work, and I had to purchase high-end dresses and keep myself meticulously manicured and groomed. I had to watch my weight and report every so often for a new profile picture. The money was good, but it was nerve-wracking dating out-of-town guys who expected me to be more than just an escort. Again, it was preferred that I didn't speak when on a date with the clients. It was understood that small talk is accepted when initiated. I had to learn to eat in the European fashion with knife and fork and to be ladylike and polite. It was acting and roleplaying. How long would it be before Hollywood discovered me?

I stood nearby while the client cajoled and conversed with his target audience. I was window dressing. It seemed like just another mild form of prostitution to me. I got a chance to play tour guide and hostess, because I knew where the nightlife was located. The pay was excellent, but the dresses and costs of maintenance were expensive.

I didn't stay in that occupation for very long, but there was one client, a fifty-five-year-old gentleman, who liked to put me in wrestling holds (the camel clutch) as foreplay. He was a generous tipper and sported a libido to match. I found myself walking bowlegged after he visited. We stayed in touch (even though it was against the rules), and he came to see me during his business travels. He always rented an expensive car and took me out for a nice dinner, show, or both before taking me up to his hotel room. He was my one and only sugar daddy.

It was an unusually cold winter in Southern California. The Santa Ana winds had suddenly died out, and the temperature plummeted from eighty down to forty-five that night. It was so chilly that I engaged my space heater and stood near it to warm my buns.

At about that time, I received a call from my dear mother, and she explained that she was leaving New York City for a bit to visit relatives in Florida. She asked if I could join her. I thought to myself, "hmmmm, perfect timing, mom." I had received a postcard from her the previous week stating that she intended to visit with relatives in Florida. An idea flashed in my head.

    I had told my dear mother how things were going. I made sure she knew I loved her and asked her if she wouldn't mind me joining her if there was room available. I didn't know Mom's side of the family in Florida that well, so I didn't want to just invite myself over. She assured me it was fine and that there would be room. She was planning to stay there on Sixteenth Street in South Beach for two weeks before returning to the apple. I told her I would join her there.

    That settled it. I decided it was time for a road trip. I was going to visit Florida, too. I had saved $585 in travel money, and I intended to make the entire trip to Florida on a shoestring budget. I didn't want to leave my apartment, but my finances were on the decline at that moment. I sold my Toyota for some quick cash and planned my Florida escape. I put some stuff in storage and energized myself, thinking Florida might be a nice place to go for a while.

Incidentally, you may have noticed that I haven't lived up to my cyber girl title yet. Not to worry—my adventures continue. In some respects, it has been an out-of-this-world experience. Stay tuned.

XOXO,
Vantessa

Printed in the United States
By Bookmasters